THE DEVIL YOU KNOW

HELL'S ANGEL BOOK THREE

JANE HINCHEY

BAYWOLF PRESS
BP
BAYWOLF PRESS

AUTHOR'S NOTE

Dear Reader,

Big news in my literary world! As you know, I've been writing as both Jane Hinchey and Zahra Stone. It's been quite the adventure, but now it's time for a change. I'm bringing everything back under my original name, Jane Hinchey. Just like my stories, life has its twists, and this is the latest one for me.

What does this mean for your Zahra Stone favorites? They're getting a fresh look with my real name, but the stories inside are the same ones you love.

As you delve into The Devil You Know, you're not just reading a story, but joining me on my author's journey. Your support has been invaluable, and I'm so grateful for it.

Here's to more mystery, more romance, and more adventures together!

xoxo

Jane

The world is burning, and I'm the one who lit the match...

I didn't mean to. In fact, I thought I was playing the hero. Turns out I got played the fool.

Betrayed by those I love most, I've gone into hiding to lick my wounds while praying things get better. Meanwhile, the earth is broken, Heaven is bleeding, and someone—or something—is trying to break the seal on Hell.

Last time, I only made things worse. This time I must do better.

I'm the CEO of Hell, so naturally it falls to me (and my sassy orange kitten sidekick) to mediate this celestial war that's been brewing for millennia. Yeah, wish me luck.

CHAPTER

ONE

The truck fishtailed as I planted my foot hard on the accelerator. Red and blue lights flashed in the rear-view mirror, lighting up the interior of the cab, and I whooped in delight. This was so much fun! Gone was the old Lucifer, always doing what was expected of her: always on the job, always saving souls. In her place was Hell-raising Lucifer, and I relished every second, for it let me forget, for brief moments, and I so desperately needed to forget. Even now, in the middle of a high-speed pursuit, memories threatened to consume me. Memories that wanted to drag me under into darkness and pain. I pushed them deep down inside, so far that they'd never see the light of day. I hoped.

The police car followed as I sped down the dirt backroads of Fury Island, the windows down, taking the corners at breakneck speeds while my hair whipped around my face. Glancing down, I grabbed my beer from the cup holder. How clever of the humans to design such a thing—a holder for your beverage of choice. I took a swig, swerved across the road, and then dropped the bottle back into the holder, regaining control of the truck.

The lights behind faded. They'd called off the pursuit.

"Pussies!" I shouted out the window. My cell phone rang, and the truck's Bluetooth picked up the call. "Yo?" I answered.

"Lucy." It was Jase. Probably wondering where his truck was.

"Do you have my truck?" He asked.

Bingo.

"Maybe." I wanted to lie and say no, but still, I had this innate compulsion to speak the truth—it was infuriating. Since leaving Heaven, I'd hidden out on Earth, subduing my angelic—or demonic—depending on how you look at it—powers by living as one with the humans. That meant no magic. The minute I used it, they'd be able to track me, for I had no doubt that Levi and Dacian were searching. Only they didn't know what realm I was on, they may suspect Earth, but where, on this vast planet, would Lucifer, the Queen of Hell, hide?

My mind was drifting dangerously close to the one man who I did not, one hundred percent, want to think about. Levi. He'd destroyed me. The human turned fire demon had done what no one, angel or demon, had ever managed. He'd gotten under my defenses: I took my guard down and opened my heart wide for him. That's when he struck, hard and fast. The memory of it still left me breathless.

"Lucy, we've talked about this."

I jumped at the sound of Jase's voice, having forgotten he was on the line.

"I'm just blowing off some steam," I protested. "You're always trying to spoil my fun." The pout in my voice was real, for I'd discovered walking on the dark side was an enjoyable activity.

"Yeah, well, can you blow off steam in your own car? Oh, that's right, you don't have one!"

"Sarcasm doesn't become you, Jase." I could picture the tall blonde vet raking his hand through his hair in frustration.

"Just bring the truck back, Lucy. The police rang, asking if I was aware it had been stolen."

"The cops are as much fun as you." I took

another swig of beer, frowning when I noticed the precariously low volume left in the bottle. Reaching over to the passenger seat, I dug around in the brown paper bag, found it empty, and cursed. I was out of booze. The tires screeched as the vehicle meandered onto the wrong side of the road. I glanced up, overcorrected, and finally managed to get the thing back under control and in the correct lane.

"Lucy!"

"Fine!" I shouted. "I'll bring your precious truck back." I disconnected the call, annoyed at Jase. Hell, I was annoyed at everyone these days. I knew Del and Jase were on eggshells around me. The only one who didn't give a damn was Duke; the black lab would ignore my lousy mood and demand I give him a pat. Just like that, with my hand stroking his luxurious fur, my mood would ease. For a while at least.

Softening at the memory, I eased off the accelerator and turned the truck back toward town. I had a shortcut the cops had yet to discover, and with not a police car in sight, I parked the car at the back of Jase's vet clinic, with no one the wiser. It was a beautiful night; the air was warm with a slight summer breeze coming off the ocean. The moonlight was unfiltered, not a cloud in the midnight sky. I sighed. How I wished it was winter, with thundering storms and cold winds lashing my body—for that was how I felt inside. It would be nice to have the weather reflect my mood, not the romantic paradise Fury Island was exhibiting.

I stood looking at the house attached to the vet clinic. It was dark, all the lights off, and I knew Jase and Del were inside sleeping. Pushing down any errant melancholy that surfaced, I swiveled on my heel and began the walk into town. I'd had my fun with the truck, but I wasn't ready for my night to be over; for then, I'd have to face the inevitable truth. I'd be going to sleep alone and waking up alone. Ever since fleeing Heaven, I'd never felt so utterly alone in my life.

The Elephant & Wheelbarrow—a wholly English pub on a Caribbean island—was my drinking venue of choice. Stepping through the rustic door was like stepping into another dimension, and I liked the irony of it. The pub smelled like old smoke, leather, and for some bizarre reason, freshly cut roses when there were no flowers to be seen.

Sliding onto what I considered my barstool, I waved at Gloria, a well-endowed woman in her forties who had a smile for everyone and white curls that bounced in total disarray around her shoulders. Some days her perpetual happiness grated on my nerves, and all I'd have to offer her was a growl. On those days, she knew it was best to leave me alone.

"What'll it be this evening, Lucy?" she asked, filling a glass with ice, then a shot of whiskey, and setting it in front of the man a few seats down.

"Sex on the beach?" I asked, tapping my fingers against my chin as I mentally scanned through the list of cocktails I'd made it my mission to devour. I'd been here a week, and this was my third rotation of the cocktail list.

Wiping her hands on a tea towel, she smiled, "Coming right up."

The man who'd ordered the whiskey moved to the barstool next to mine and nudged me with his elbow. "I can help with that," he said.

"What?" I knew what was coming. Always did. Stupid humans.

He grinned, raking his hand through his hair. "Sex on the beach."

I glanced at him, only to be rewarded with a leer. So gross. "Not interested." Ignoring him, I turned to Gloria, who was making my cocktail. She looked from me to the guy and back again, trying not to smile.

"No need to be rude," he puffed, and my eyebrows shot into my hairline.

"Rude? Dude, that was not rude. Your pathetic attempt to have sex with me was declined. You take rejection as rude? No. You see, this is where human nature has gone all wrong. Men feel entitled. They feel they can say and do what they want to a woman with no consequences. When a woman says no, she's rude, or a bitch, or frigid, or whatever other insults you think you can throw at her. But you know what? I don't give a rat's ass what you think. Say what you want. Honestly, I don't care because you mean nothing to me—your existence has no meaning in my life whatsoever. I'm meant to feel privileged that you deigned to speak to me? Well, here's some advice for you. Go fuck yourself, you pathetic twat waffle."

Gloria barked out a laugh, slid the cocktail to me, and addressed the guy who was now flushed bright red. "You lucked out, Pete, move along now, and stop bothering the lady."

"She ain't no lady," he protested, grabbing his drink and scampering away. I wanted to read him, to open my magic and see if he was slated for

Heaven or Hell, but I'd suppressed those abilities since arriving on Fury Island, and the not-knowing was liberating. I got to judge every person I met on the merits of how I perceived them to be at that moment, not what I knew of their past. I'm sure many of them were sinners, some worse than others, but I enjoyed not knowing, not judging. Sweet, sweet, freedom.

TWO

I was eventually kicked out of the Elephant & Wheelbarrow when it closed. Still, I wasn't ready to go home even though I could barely stand up, fatigue and alcohol making me stumble as I staggered out the door. Outside I squinted into the darkness, my eyes refusing to adjust. Rubbing them with my fists, I repeatedly blinked before my focus returned. While I was on Earth, I needed to rest more, sleep more, be more human than angel, but I resisted. For when I closed my eyes, that's when Levi crept into my thoughts, and I'd wonder about him. What he was doing. If he was okay. And then I'd be angry because I cared. So, I avoided sleep as much as possible.

Instead, in the early hours of the morning, while

the rest of Fury Island was sleeping, I walked the shores, wandering aimlessly until the sun rose over the horizon, and I eventually stumbled into my bed in Del's old cottage. Now that she'd moved in with Jase, her place was empty, and she'd agreed to let me be her tenant.

I was down on the beach when raucous laughter echoed on the night air, and in the distance, flames shot toward the sky. I assumed someone had set up a campfire on the beach and headed in that direction when the mewing of a kitten froze the blood in my veins. I paused for a second, then sprinted forward, my gaze zeroing in on three teenagers standing around the campfire, laughing. One of them held a tiny orange kitten by the scruff, dangling it over the flames. It twisted and meowed in fear while the boys laughed and taunted it, lowering it closer to the flame before pulling it back.

Then the unthinkable happened. The teenager holding the kitten let it go. Without hesitation, I extended my wings and froze time, snatching the kitten up in my hand before the flames could touch it. With it cradled against my chest, time resumed, and the boys looked at me in horror, my wings of fire spread out behind me, my eyes dancing with the horrors of Hell.

"Run," I boomed, for I was ready to consume their souls then and there for what they'd done. They didn't need telling twice. They dropped but bottle of beer they'd been holding and ran, scrambling and tripping in their haste. With their backs to me, I flung out a hand, marking them, one, two, three. Hell was now in their future.

The kitten meowed against me, and I ran a soothing hand over its trembling back, healing any burns it had received with a stroke of my hand.

"There now," I soothed, keeping my voice low and concealing my wings, "that's better, isn't it?" The kitten began purring, and I smiled. Then I realized what I'd done. I'd used my magic. They'd have seen. I needed to get out of here now. Hugging the kitten to my chest, I took off at a jog, making sure my magic was locked down tight. I couldn't be angry for risking it; the little ball of orange fluff cradled against my chest was worth it. I'd have to stay vigilant, keep out of sight, and maybe I'd get lucky and wouldn't be discovered. I almost laughed at the impossibility of my hopes.

They'd be looking alright. Not only Levi, my fated mate, but possibly Dacian, one of my oldest friends. Then there was Dad, God, the one who'd done the unthinkable and then hid it from me. But he'd been in the predicament he was in because of my mom, Lilith. And they'd all be looking for me. And let's not forget Ashliel, my second in command. I'd left her looking after Hell—she'd be concerned by now. I usually checked in regularly. To be silent for so long was not like me, and I knew she'd be worried. My thoughts briefly touched on my brothers Gabriel and Michael, banished to Earth for their sins. Not that they'd be looking. They didn't know the latest. Plus, they were assholes. If they were looking for me, it would be to laugh and poke fun at my expense.

Arriving home breathless and wheezing, I unlocked the door and staggered inside. Putting the kitten on the floor, I leaned over, hands on knees, trying to catch my breath. I'd run the entire way from the beach to the cottage. Uphill. Fuck, I was out of shape. I poured myself a glass of water in the kitchen before putting a saucer of milk down for the kitten. It continued purring as it lapped it up.

My phone began ringing, and I glanced at the screen. It was Del.

"What happened? I felt something," she demanded as soon as I answered the call.

"I slipped. Used some magic."

Silence greeted my words. Then she said, cautiously, "And?"

"And now I'm hiding."

"What made you use magic?"

"Some idiot kids were about to drop a kitten into a bonfire."

Her gasp echoed my sentiments exactly. "Oh, God. Is it okay? Did you save it?"

"Yes, it's okay. I have it here. She was a little singed, but I healed her."

"Oh, Lucy."

"Save it." I knew where she was going with this. Del had a soft heart. She wanted me to reach out to Levi, to talk to him, but I refused. "I don't want to talk about it. Can you get Jase to come by and check on the kitten?"

"I thought you said you healed it?"

"I did, but I want him to take a look. Make sure it's okay."

"You're keeping it, aren't you?" I knew she was smiling, since I could hear it in her voice, so I hung up. Del was good to me. Patient and kind, and I repaid her by being rude and mean. I couldn't help it. Everyone and everything irritated me these days.

Del, Jase, and their dog Duke were...special. They were the key to the gates of Hell. The key had started off as a single talisman. Over time, it was broken into three pieces and scattered to the corners of the globe, entrusted to select people for safekeeping. Only, it was getting harder and harder to keep a relic hidden, these humans could be tenacious when they wanted to be, and with a demon hot on the trail and a shard of the relic in Del's hands, I'd transformed the key. It was now an intrinsic part of Del, Jase, and Duke, evident by the tattoo's the three of them bore. Collectively, they were the key. Hidden. Secure.

They were the reason I was on Fury Island. They shielded me from any location spells Levi or my dad may have used to find me. And with my magic locked down, I intended to stay hidden until I was ready to face them on my own terms. Right now, I was rubbed raw. I was too angry at my father for unknowingly absorbing my unborn child to save himself and at Levi, who had known and not told me. I felt like a first-class idiot for not even knowing I was pregnant—granted, my baby had only been conceived hours earlier. Still, Levi had sensed the moment our daughter had sprung into creation. And he hadn't said a word!

Silent tears tracked down my cheeks, and I swiped them away. I'd lost her before I'd had the chance to celebrate her. My daughter. Levi and I hadn't even talked about kids yet, but when a being chose you as her parents, boom, you were knocked up whether you wanted to be or not.

The kitten mewed, and I crouched, scooping it up and cradling it against my chest. It yawned, and I followed suit. It was time to sleep. I'd worry about the rest later. Climbing the stairs, I slid under the covers fully clothed with the kitten tucked under my chin, its purr vibrating through my chest. Together, we slept.

THREE

It was barely two hours later when a bang on the door jolted me awake.

"Seriously?" I grumbled, eyes bleary. Throwing back the covers, I scooped up the kitten, tucked it under one arm, and stumbled down the stairs, half asleep. I could sense who was on the other side of the door before I opened it.

"A house call," I muttered. "I'm honored."

"Del told me you have a new house guest." Jase smiled his wide smile, dazzling me with his teeth, and pushed past me, his arms full. "I've brought supplies. Litter tray. Food. Vaccinations."

Pushing the door shut, I waited while Jase set up the litter tray, took the kitten from me, and placed it inside. The poor little thing must have been bursting, for it immediately squatted and took a pee.

"Plumbing's working ok," Jase observed, moving on to the food. Scooping something wet and foul looking into a bowl, he placed it on the floor. Once the kitten had finished scratching around in the tray, it clambered out, tripped, smacked its face on the floor, shook itself, then continued straight for the food. It purred as it ate.

"I'm a bad pet parent," I confessed. I'd given it milk, but nothing else.

"Don't be ridiculous," Jase scolded. "You rescued it hours ago. Where were you going to find all this at four in the morning?"

"I told Del I'd bring it in for a check. You didn't have to come." Annoyance tinged my words, the heat of my ever-burning anger not far beneath the surface.

"Lucy," he sighed. We'd been butting heads ever since I arrived on Fury Island. Everything he said, I automatically disagreed with. It wasn't that I didn't like him. He was a good man, and I wouldn't have chosen him to be a part of the key if he wasn't. To be honest, arguing with him had become more habit than anything else.

"Del is coming over later with some toys and bedding. I just brought the essentials. Once she's finished eating, I'll look at her, give her shots, and be out of your hair."

Right. Let's ignore that I sounded like an unreasonable and ungrateful bitch.

"Coffee?" I asked instead of giving him the apology he was probably expecting. Or maybe he wasn't. He was probably used to my crappy moods by now.

"Sure," he said.

I made coffee while Jase watched the kitten. I thought he was being creepy weird, but he explained that he was observing her to make sure she could eat and swallow okay and that she didn't have trouble walking. Once she finished stuffing her face, she sat back and began grooming herself. At first, she did an absolute crap job, but instinct had her licking her tiny paw and rubbing it against her face. Cutest thing ever.

Jase laid a towel over the kitchen table, opened his vet bag, and pulled out a stethoscope, thermometer, and syringe. Then he scooped the kitten up and placed it on the towel. And just like that, my eyes welled up. The tiny kitten looked impossibly small in comparison to his big hands—it was just a baby. A baby.

Not wanting him to see my distress, I left my coffee on the bench and bolted upstairs with no word of explanation. I needed a shower. I'd been in these clothes for three days now, and I'm sure I smelled delightful...too bad I didn't care.

Staring at my reflection in the bathroom mirror, I grimaced. Still as beautiful as ever. If you looked close enough, the only thing that was different was the dullness in my eyes. To me, they were flat. Lifeless. They reflected the pain and despair from my fight with Levi and the loss of my baby, and I wondered if I'd ever get over it. Would it always hurt this much?

Stripping off my clothes, I stepped beneath the spray of the shower, contemplating the day ahead. First, get rid of Jase. Although I was grateful he'd come to check on the kitten and bring it what it needed, Del would turn up soon—I'm surprised she didn't come with Jase—then I'd have to put up with her good-natured concern. But, once I booted her out, the day was my own. Only I was spending it on lockdown. The slip with my magic last night meant I might have led Levi and whoever else was with him straight to Fury Island. The tv and couch sounded awesome right now, and my mind ran through the daytime soaps I found quite entertaining. And of course, I had the kitten to keep me company, so Del could stop worrying so damn much.

Coming back downstairs dressed in track pants, a t-shirt, and fuzzy socks, I felt marginally better. Nothing would take away the constant ache in my chest, but the sight of the little orange ball of fluff sitting at the bottom of the stairs certainly eased it.

"Hey," I cooed, picking up the kitten and cuddling her. "How about some tv, huh? We're having a quiet day in, fuzzy butt." Flopping on the couch, I picked up the remote and flicked through the channels until I found something appealing. *I Love Lucy* appeared on the screen, and I snorted. How appropriate. Settling back, the kitten turned in circles on my lap before settling into a position.

Lucy's re-runs were interrupted with the arrival of Del. I called out to come in before she even reached the door.

"It's so freaky when you do that," she said in greeting as Duke ambled inside. Carrying two bags, she pushed the door shut and followed the black lab.

"Told you, I can sense you, Jase, and Duke."

Duke sniffed the air, tail wagging. First, he explored the kitchen and then sniffed his way to me, zeroing in on the kitten on my lap. I expected the kitten to hiss and spit; instead, she looked at Duke and then stretched her neck to sniff. Nose to nose, the two got acquainted.

"Oh, my God," Del squealed, "that's just the sweetest thing I've ever seen."

"Yeah, yeah." I put the kitten on the floor, keeping a close eye in case Duke trod on her...or worse, decided she was a tasty morsel.

"You don't have to worry about Duke," Del said as if reading my mind. "He's great with all animals. He's a big softie, wants to mother them all."

"So, Jase left when I was in the shower, and I didn't get to ask, is the kitten a girl or boy?" Although I'd been referring to the kitten as a girl, I hadn't been sure.

"She's a girl." Del sat in the armchair to my right and began digging around in the bags she'd brought with her. Out came a mountain of cat toys. I smiled at her indulgence.

"Have you thought of a name yet?" she asked, pulling out a cat bed that had been scrunched up tight inside the bag. It exploded once released from its confines. She threw it at me, and I caught it one-handed and tossed it onto the floor.

"Nah." I shrugged. I guess I should name her but thinking of girl names brought me back to my lost little girl, and my brain froze.

"Are you okay?" Del paused what she was doing and looked at me with concern. My throat was tight, so tight that I couldn't force out a single word. Still, I managed to nod.

"Your baby, the one you lost, was a girl?" She knew the basics and had been diligently pecking away at me ever since I arrived to get the whole story.

I nodded again.

"We should do something for her," Del said. "A memorial. A way for you to say goodbye."

"Stop." I did not want to talk about this. At all. Ever.

"Please talk to Levi. He must be hurting, too. The two of you can support each other."

"Stop." This time there was a thread of steel in my tone mixed with a layer of anger. She needed to stop pushing. I was holding on by a thread. If she pushed me over the edge, it wouldn't be pretty.

"Lucy, I know you're hurting. I can see your pain, and it makes me hurt. You say you can sense me?

Well, I can sense you, too, and I have to be honest, it hasn't been pleasant. You came here to get your head together and heal, but you've done nothing —*nothing*—to help yourself. You've been stealing cars, holding parties in people's houses who are out of town, getting drunk almost every night. It's not helping."

She opened her mouth to continue, but I held up a hand and shouted, "Enough!" The whole house shook, Duke whimpered, and the kitten ran to him, seeking shelter between his front paws. Remorse washed over me. I didn't want to scare the kitten or Duke, they were innocents in this, but I couldn't let Del keep pushing. For if she broke through, I'd unravel. I doubted I'd be able to put myself back together. I couldn't risk it.

"Lucy ..."

I glared her into silence. "I swear, Del, I don't want to hurt you, but you have to shut the fuck up. I. Do. Not. Want. To. Talk. About. It." I breathed out and tried to still the tremble rocking my body. "Please, just go."

"I'm sorry," she whispered, biting down on her bottom lip.

I swallowed my emotions. I knew she meant well, but this was one of those things that I had to deal with in my own way. Which at the moment was avoidance.

I NAMED the kitten Nibbler because she chewed on everything. The TV cords. My shoes. An old magazine I'd tossed on the floor when I'd finished reading it. Her toys. She was insatiable with her little razor teeth, so Nibbler it was.

The next couple of days were spent in glorious solitude, just Nibbler and me. Del and Jase stayed away, and no one turned up on Fury Island looking for me. Life was surprisingly good, and with each passing day, my guard lowered, I relaxed, and began to heal.

Then it turned to shit. It started when Del, Jase, and Duke turned up on my doorstep, uninvited. I knew from the glowing tattoo inside Duke's ear that something terrible had happened.

"Don't tell me," I drawled, "your tattoos are glowing, too?"

"Yes. And they're kinda warm and tingly. What does it mean?" Del was rubbing at her chest where her tattoo was hidden beneath her clothes.

"It means someone is trying to break into, or out

of, Hell." I sighed. "Vacation over. Look after Nibbler for me, will you? I've gotta go kick someone's ass."

Kissing the top of Nibbler's head, I handed her over to Del, reluctant to part with her. "I'll be back," I whispered, then spread my wings and disappeared, reappearing moments later in Hell HQ.

FOUR

ell HQ was a black marble skyscraper perched precariously on the very edge of my realm, towering up over the city on one side and down into eternal darkness on the other. My penthouse was on the top floor with my offices immediately below. I hadn't realized until I returned that I'd actually missed it. The sleek surfaces, glass walls, the hustle and bustle of my demons patrolling the streets and skies, keeping my realm safe. And then there was my second in command: Ashliel.

"Finally!" Ashliel glanced over her shoulder at me, her flaming locks moving over her shoulders like molten lava. "Where the Hell have you been?"

"On vacation." Striding forward, I stood in front of the wall of monitors and scanned them. "What's up?"

"Nothing, why?" She was typing on her electronic clipboard. "Is something meant to be wrong?"

"I got an alert that someone is trying to break in. Or out."

Throwing her head back, she laughed. "Break into Hell? As if." She snorted and smiled to herself.

"So...no alarms on this side? Nothing unusual?"

She studied me intently before turning her attention to the screens. "Nothing obvious, no. No alarms triggered on this side, but how were you alerted? That might factor into it."

"The key activated," I said.

"Not good," she growled, all business now.

Standing shoulder to shoulder, we scrolled through the screens, monitoring every inch of Hell. Nothing seemed out of place.

"Initiate a lockdown. I want Hell searched from top to bottom. If there is a breach, I want to know about it. The attempt must have come from the outside; someone was trying to get in, not out. Otherwise, this board would be lit up with alarms.

Nevertheless, we're not taking any chances. Full lockdown, search, and then increase patrols."

Ashliel hurried off to do my bidding, and I stood, looking out over my domain. *My domain.* But of course, this is where it happened, in the mountain ranges on the horizon, the hidden chamber where my mother had imprisoned my father for eons. Then, we stumbled upon him. To save himself, he drained my magic to fuel his own; only he'd accidentally swept up the essence of my daughter, effectively ending my pregnancy. The pain I'd been trying to bury for the last week erupted with an intensity that stole my breath. Tears filled my eyes, blurring my vision, as my heart yearned for what was lost.

"Gah, Lucifer, pull yourself together," Ashliel snapped, her heels clipping across the floor. "Your energy is choking. You want payback? Drag their sorry asses into the pit and be done with it."

I snorted. Ash was always a sharpshooter. She had no time for bullshit or emotion. I glanced at her. The green of her eyes sparkled like freshly cut emeralds. Hard and sharp.

"Anyway, I think I found the problem." She handed me the clipboard.

"What am I looking at?" I asked with a frown.

"Geez, did someone give you a lobotomy while you were on vacation?" she snapped, her irritation evident.

Now I knew how people felt around me. Intimidated and keen to get away from the bad-tempered dragon I'd become.

"Ash," I reprimanded, matching her tone. "You've done a brilliant job here, and I applaud you for it, but there are boundaries—my dear—and you are skating precariously close to the edge."

My gaze drilled into hers, and we battled silently until she lowered hers. A grin spread across her face. "Welcome back, Lucifer."

Handing back the clipboard, I turned my attention to the wall of monitors. "This has to be the work of Lilith," I said to myself.

"Armageddon?" Ash suggested, one brow arched.

"Could be." I nodded. Earth was in trouble. Serious trouble. Simultaneously, across the globe, volcanoes erupted, earthquakes tore apart cities and highways, and tsunamis roared through the oceans. All of the Earth's fault lines were on the move.

"The triggering of the key was a trick, wasn't it?" Ashliel asked.

"Yeah. She wanted me out of the way. Off Earth, so she could launch her attack."

"But why?"

"Because she wants to hurt Dad any way she can, and her focus right now is the Earth he created. Has she forgotten her sons have been banished there? That she's risking their lives in her drive for revenge?"

Ashliel cocked her head. "Cold."

"As ice." I sighed. "I'm going to have to fix this, aren't I?" We both stood, waiting in the hope that God would appear earthside and put an end to the destruction Lilith was raining down. Alas, there was no sign of dear old Dad.

"Looks like it. Off you go, I'll continue to manage things here."

Dismissed by Ash, I returned to Fury Island, my temporary home away from home.

"Lucy, thank God!" Del grabbed my arm and jerked me toward the front door of the cottage. "You have to do something. You have to stop it!"

Placing my hands over Del's, I halted her. "Stop what?"

"A tsunami, heading straight for us. It will wipe Fury Island off the map."

"Goddamit," I cursed. Twisting my hair into a

knot on top of my head, I secured it with a band. Shrugging out of my jacket, I tossed it at Del and cracked my knuckles. I had work to do.

"Where's Nibbler?" I asked. I needed to know they were all safe before I left, knowing I wouldn't be able to focus if I was worried about this lot. Glancing around, I spotted the tiny ball of fluff curled up between Duke's front paws.

I pointed to Del and Jase. "The four of you have to stay in this house. No matter what you hear outside, do not open the door. Understood?"

"Why? What are you going to do?" Jase wrapped his fingers around Del's and squeezed.

"I'm going to protect this house; then I'm going to stop the shit show that is going on right now. The tsunami is just the beginning. This problem is global."

"But...wh...how?" Del was lost for words. Her eyes revealed her distress.

"I don't have time to explain. All you need to know is that I can keep you safe if you stay inside. Even if the tsunami hits, you'll be safe. You might be floating in a house in the ocean, but you'll be safe. The house will hold. Open the door, and you're doomed. And let me tell you, I'll be pissed if anything happens to any of you, including Nibbler. Keep the door closed. Understood?"

"Yes," they replied in unison. Closing my eyes, I summoned my magic, drawing from the Earth itself to cast a protective bubble around the cottage.

Using that much power gave me a heady rush. I strode out of the house with a new pep in my step. I knew using that much magic would be like a beacon, leading Levi right to me, but that seemed inconsequential to what was happening around me.

The air outside was still, deadly still. Not even a bird chirped. The leaves didn't dare rustle.

I rushed down to the foreshore and stood on the beach, amazed at the sight before me. The water was gone. Sucked out, the empty ocean floor stretched for miles. I knew what was coming, though; all that water was going to come rushing back, with a vengeance, destroying anything in its path.

Fury Island would not survive the onslaught.

I felt him before I saw him, the familiar warmth of his energy mere feet away. I refused to turn around; instead, I kept my gaze on the horizon. The water would be returning soon, and I had to be ready. I had one shot at saving the island.

"Lucy." His voice was music to my ears and, simultaneously, a stake through my heart.

"Now's not the time, Levi," I whispered, barely able to get the words out.

"Can we assume this is Lilith's doing?" Dacian asked from behind my left shoulder.

I nodded, "You can. Is Dad here?"

"Not yet," Dacian replied.

I risked a glance at Dacian, Dad's right-hand angel, and my best friend. "He is coming, isn't he? He is planning to help? Because this is just one tsunami. I cannot save the entire planet."

Resting a hand on my shoulder, Dacian reassured me. "My army is here to assist, and you have Levi and me."

I snorted. "It won't be enough. Lilith is too powerful. And what of Michael and Gabriel? They were banished to Earth to live as humans. They will be powerless to save themselves, let alone assist us."

"I'm sorry, Lucy, I just don't know," Dacian admitted, and the anger that had been simmering beneath the surface heated to a steady boil. Fuck my parents. This was all their fault. If they could sort their shit out and learn to get along, none of this would be happening. And the last thing I wanted was to be dragged into the middle of their domestic affairs—Heaven only knows, I had my own problems.

"It's coming," Levi said. He was behind me, off to the right. I glanced at him, my gaze thirsty for a peek. My breath hitched in my throat. He looked... ragged. Exhausted. Tired and fed up. He looked how I felt.

"What's wrong with you?" I blurted, breaking my rule of not speaking to him ever again.

"Oh, you know, been searching the Universe for my mate, who thought it would be fun to play hide and seek." He hissed the words at me through clenched teeth. Now he was angry at me. *At me!* The nerve.

"Fun?" I screeched. "Fun is the last thing I've been having, Levi Forrester!" I bellowed, my voice echoing around us.

"Guys.... GUYS!" Dacian interjected before we could get into it any further. "Look!"

Levi and I turned our heads. A wall of water over a hundred feet high was barreling toward Fury Island. It would hit in a matter of minutes.

"Holy shit," Levi whispered, cracking his knuckles, and stretching his neck from side to side, readying for battle.

"Spread out," I ordered, flinging my arms out to

indicate to Dacian and Levi to position themselves along the beach on either side of me. My wings spread out at full width behind me. I wasn't sure we'd be able to pull this off. Dacian and I could fly out of danger, but Levi couldn't. If he got swept up in the wave, there would be no saving him. With my heart thundering in my chest, I glanced over at him. A surge of adrenaline warmed my blood. He met my gaze, his love for me blazing like a laser beam straight into my heart.

This was what I was afraid of. Seeing him again. Falling for him all over again, after he'd hurt me so badly. Even as the thoughts tumbled through my head and the tsunami barreled towards us, I remembered how Levi made me feel. And despite everything, seeing him now reminded me of how much I loved him, how the ache of being apart was unrelenting. Damn it.

"Now!" Dacian yelled.

Without thought, I pushed out my power. Sweeping my arms wide, I pushed an invisible wall up against the swell of water. It pushed back. Hard.

Grunting, I staggered one step back and then two. Levi and Dacian were doing the same, our combined power hopefully enough to turn back the tide. Digging my heels in, I held my ground, wincing when I was pushed farther back, my feet digging channels in the sand. We were losing ground. Sweat beaded on my upper lip, and my arms trembled from the effort.

"Fuck," Dacian swore.

I knew what he was thinking. We were going to lose. Fury Island was seconds away from being obliterated, thanks to Lilith. The spark of anger that had been boiling beneath my skin exploded at the thought of what she had done. Fuck her. It was time to take that bitch down.

"Yarrrrghhhhh!" I screamed, putting all my fury into it, channeling everything I had. All the pent-up emotion, wild and feral within me, came spewing out, unguarded and intense. I was raw with it, exposed and vulnerable, but I didn't notice or care. I had to save the island.

"It's working!" Dacian shouted. "Keep going."

With a final frenzy of power, we beat it. The giant wall of water slammed to the ocean floor with a thunderous crash, droplets shooting high into the sky and raining down on us. I was euphoric in our victory and turned to Dacian with a grin on my face.

"We did it." Dacian cheered, slapping me on the back. I stared at my best friend, sobering.

"It's not over. There are earthquakes, volcanic

eruptions, cyclones, you name it. Lilith is raining it down on Earth. I shudder to think how many have died already."

Dacian nodded his agreement. "The only way to stop this is to stop Lilith."

"Duh." Spinning on my heel, I trudged back toward the cottage.

"Lucy, wait," Levi called, jogging to catch up with me. I didn't stop, but I didn't protest when he matched his steps to mine, keeping pace.

"I'm sorry." He said. "For everything."

"I'm sure you are."

He tried to take my hand, but I snatched it away.

"Lucy, please."

His begging was almost my undoing. Almost. But then Dacian jumped in front of me, blocking my path.

"Lucifer, far be it for me to interfere with your love life, but someone needs to. I've been saddled with sad-sack here for the last week, and to say it's depressing would be an understatement. You two need to sit down and have a conversation. Communicate. What happened was an absolute tragedy, it really was, but Lucy? It wasn't Levi's fault."

"He should have told me." My hurt was real, and while I knew what Dacian said was true, it didn't stop the hurt from hurting.

"Yes. He should have. But he didn't. And I bet he's wishing with every molecule of his being that he could turn back the clock and have a do-over." Dacian waved an arm toward Levi, who was nodding so hard it was almost comical. "But none of us have that luxury. The best he can do is beg forgiveness and move on. How about channeling some of that fury and hate towards the person who is actually responsible for all of this?"

"Lilith," I supplied, my anger once more seething beneath the surface, making my skin prickle and the hairs on the back of my neck stand up. Sucking in a deep breath, I filled my lungs then slowly breathed out, closing my fingers into fists.

"Exactly. There is no one but her to blame for all of this."

I digested what he said, knew he spoke the truth. Had I become bitter and twisted, incapable of forgiveness, like my mother? The thought horrified me. Dacian read it in my face and smiled gently, caressed my cheek.

"I'm going to check on the key. You two talk."

Dacian began to walk up the hill toward the cottage. My head threatened to spin off my shoulders.

"He's right," I whispered, finally facing Levi head-on. "We need to talk."

CHAPTER
FIVE

"Come on bitch, deal or fold?" The woman sitting opposite me snarled.

I glanced at the cards in my hand. The two of hearts and seven of spades. Definitely not a winning hand. Lowering the cards face down on the table, I pushed my chips forward, adding them to the mountain-sized pile in the middle of the poker table.

My lips curled. "All in," I replied.

Her lips thinned into a straight line, and one eye twitched. The room around us was dim. A single light bulb dangled overhead, shedding enough light to illuminate our table before falling away into shadows. We were in an illegal gambling den in a dirty back alley of Redmeadows, where the desperate came to try and win a fortune, and the sharks consumed them.

Only hours earlier, Levi and I had been on Fury Island battling a Tsunami. With that particular disaster taken care of, we'd talked. He'd apologized, wholeheartedly, and I'd forgiven him, but the question lingered in my mind... could I forget? And that's when I'd received word from Ashliel that swarms of flies were descending in Redmeadows and she didn't think it was a natural phenomenum.

Returning my attention to the woman across from me, I waited. The ball was in her court. The rest of the table was out. Despite Levi's psychic abilities when he was human, they hadn't done him any favors today, and he'd folded early. Alongside him was a retired judge who'd burned through his retirement fund and was here, selling his soul for the off chance of redemption. He found none in this room.

Then there was the desperate husband, who kept spinning his wedding ring around and around on his finger. He'd strayed. Cheated on his wife and was being blackmailed. They had pictures and were threatening to send them to his wife if he didn't pay up. His savings were gone, leaving this room his last resort. He was about to lose it all.

And then there was the cocky young man who believed he was about to win his fortune. After all, lady luck had always been his friend. Sadly for him, this wasn't a place where luck would find him.

I knew all of this because I knew them. I knew their stories. I knew the things they'd done, the sins they'd committed. I usually spent my time on Earth trying to steer humans back on to the right path, to atone for their sins before they end up in Hell. But this visit was different. This time, I'm not steering. I'm hunting. My vacation on Fury Island was well and truly over when Lilith released her wrath. We'd managed the earthquakes, tsunamis, and volcanoes. So she upped the ante, releasing creatures from another realm onto Earth to run amok. I was here to send them back.

Which brings me back to the woman across from me, the one hiding behind a human facade. But I saw her. The *real* her. Outside, thunder rumbled, adding to the somber mood in the room. The darkness circled us, curling up around my legs, billowing like a mist across the room, and then hiding in the shadows, waiting. Her control was slipping. She couldn't stay hidden for much longer.

Outside, the wind whistled and buffeted the building. What sounded like a crack of lightning rang out, but the buzz of the insects was louder. Heads swiveled to the windows covered by black plastic to keep the world unaware of what went on in this room.

"Deal or fold," I challenged. Silence echoed between us, the table trembled, and several startled gasps rang out.

"Lucy," Levi hissed in warning.

I ignored him. Did he think I didn't know what I was doing? Did he think I didn't know who this was? For across from me, wearing a human disguise, was the female death spirit, Keres. Her entourage of insects gave her away. She was here to bring disease to Earth with her bow and arrow, and in this room, she was building her army by fooling the desperate into doing her bidding.

Her facade shimmered, revealing her identity. She squeezed her eyes shut, and the mask snapped back in place, leaving no one the wiser. No one except me. The air was thick with tension, and I tilted my head, considering. Did she know who I was and that she wasn't getting out of this room alive?

"Well?" I arched a brow. "Seems to me like you don't have a winning hand there."

Thunder boomed, and the whole room shook. My hand was crappy, but my bluff was exemplary.

Keres slapped her cards down on the table and snarled, "I'm out."

Leaning forward, I wrapped my arms around the pile of chips, dragging them toward me. "Thanks for the game, people."

"Wait!" Keres barked, her features once more shimmering between human and the curse that she was. She rose so fast that her chair tipped over, and heads swung in her direction. All pretense at being human fled as her true self was revealed.

She was as magnificent and terrifying as you'd expect her to be. Larger than any human at seven feet tall, the top of her head brushed the ceiling. Dressed in a silver breastplate that covered her chest and fastened around her midriff, leather straps ran across her shoulders while another piece of armor was strung around her hips. The look was topped off by a bow and arrow clutched in one hand.

A sight to behold, if gnashing teeth and claws didn't put you off.

Chairs clattered as those seated at the table stood up in a panic. Keres ignored them, and with a wave of a cape made of fur, she vanished.

"Where did she go?" Levi stood alert, legs braced, ready for action.

"Take care of them." I nodded toward the stunned onlookers and then flew outside to the alley where I knew Keres would be waiting.

"Who are you?" she demanded, voice booming. Overhead, insects dipped and swayed in a black cloud, their hum almost deafening.

"I'm disappointed you don't recognize me," I yelled over the noise, slowly unfurling my burning wings behind me.

"Lucifer." Keres nodded as if confirming to herself what she suspected all along.

"What are you doing here, Keres?"

"Lilith opened the door."

"Tell me something I don't know." It was no surprise that my mother was now opening doors between dimensions. Keres may be the first to visit this realm, but she wouldn't be the last. My mother was intent on inflicting as much pain and suffering as she could.

"Fresh blood is appealing. A realm that has always been denied to us?" She parked her hands on her hips, and the fur cape blew out behind her. "It will fall at my hands." She looked like a cross between an Amazon and a Bear. The curves and sexual allure of the female warriors combined with the claws and teeth of a brutal animal.

"You know I can't allow that to happen." I pulled my flaming sword from between my wings and held it in front of me, ready for battle.

"You're too late. It's destined. The calling of the witnesses has begun, and it cannot be stopped."

"Calling of the witnesses?" I frowned. I'd never heard of it before and made a mental note to ask Ashliel about it.

"With or without me, this world shall fall." She looked apologetic. Almost. If it wasn't for the evil twist of her smirk and the darkness that curled around her.

"What does that..." I was cut off by an arrow heading straight for me. Dodging out of the way, I charged, but she was damn fast, dancing out of range time after time. Around and around, we spun, lunging and feigning. Arrows rained down on me, but I deflected each one with my sword. Her approach was smart, for all the while I was defending, I couldn't attack, but it ultimately meant we were at a catch-22. She couldn't get past my defenses, and I couldn't end this.

We'd drawn the attention of the humans, which wasn't surprising given the plague of insects that had descended on the city. The men from the card game burst through the door and into the alley. Levi's voice echoed in my ears, trying to get them back inside to safety. Despite his efforts, a crowd had gathered around us. Bet they didn't expect to see a Death Spirit and Lucifer, Queen of Hell, battling it out. A cloud of insects dropped low, buzzing around their heads, and they ran, scattering for shelter, arms wrapped around their heads.

The distractions cost me. An arrow slipped past and found its mark, embedding in my shoulder. Levi yelled my name, but I ignored him. I couldn't afford another distraction. Sucking in a pained breath, I wrenched the arrow out and winced. Blood gushed down my arm.

"That fucking hurt," I spat, anger fueling me.

I doubled down on my efforts with the sword, forcing Keres down the alley. Only it was in the wrong direction. She cast a glance over her shoulder, calculated how far she had to travel, and before I could blink, she spun, her cape fanned out, and she was gone.

I ran to the end of the alley and stood panting, blood staining my shirt as I searched for Keres, but there was no sign of her. Placing a hand on my shoulder, I healed myself, drawing out the toxins her poison arrow had delivered.

Securing my sword back between my wings, I folded them away and adjusted my jacket. Nothing more I could do here. The plague of insects lifted, and everything returned to normal.

For now, at least.

I began walking, each step taking me farther from the illegal gambling den. The alley stunk like wet dog. I didn't need to mark the men that had been at the game. They knew. They'd seen, and this time there would be no erasing their memories. The world needed to know what was coming and needed to be prepared. Lilith was on the warpath.

Levi's voice rang out to me. "Lucy! Are you alright?"

I glanced at him over my shoulder and nodded. "I'm fine."

He jogged to catch up, then got in front of me and jogged backward, so he was facing me. "Are you sure? That looked like it hurt."

"It did, but like I said, I'm fine. I healed myself." His eyes drifted to my shoulder, and I cursed when I noticed the bloodstain there. I'd forgotten to clean my clothing. On an irritated sigh, I waved my hand over the area, and the fabric was pristine once more. "There, all fixed," I told him.

"Look." He blew out a breath, chewed on his lower lip for a moment before continuing. "I know we talked and sorted things out—sort of—but I'm getting the feeling you're holding back. You haven't really forgiven me, despite wanting to."

I stopped walking and looked at him. "You're right. I want to. I'm trying to. I just need time. And with all of this going on..." I indicated the alley behind us. "I've kinda got a lot on my mind."

"You're right," he took my hand in his, entwining our fingers, and I looked at the rosy hue of my skin against the bronze ruggedness of his. Slowly I disengaged, letting my hand drop.

I expanded my wings and took flight. My time on Earth was up. I'd done what I needed to do, and while I could waste my time searching for Lilith and Keres, I chose to return to Hell and regroup. It was a fool who rushed into battle unprepared.

My head throbbed, and my tongue felt like I'd been cleaning the floor with it. Cracking open an eye, I squinted against the light streaming into my room.

"Urgh." I groaned. Rolling onto my back, I flung my arm across my eyes to block the light.

"Mrmm 'k?"

"Ashliel?" I cracked open an eye. The mound next to me moved, throwing the covers back to reveal a tangle of flaming red hair. A hand came up, pushing the hair away to reveal the face of my second in command.

"What time is it?" she muttered, running a hand over her face.

"Dunno. Morning?" Now that I was awake, one

thing became pressingly apparent. I needed to pee. Throwing the covers back, I sat up, swinging my feet to the floor. The sudden movement didn't help the throbbing in my head. Still wearing my clothes from last night, I shuffled to the bathroom, my reflection telling me I did indeed look as hungover as I felt. My long hair was a massive tangle around my head, my makeup smeared over my face. It seemed like I'd managed to spill more than one drink down my shirt.

After taking care of my bladder, I stripped and stepped into the shower, trying to remember last night's events. I'd been knocking back scotch when Ashliel had turned up, pizza in one hand, a bottle of wine in the other. "You mentioned the Apocalypse?"

She'd been possibly over-excited at the prospect. We'd eaten the pizza, drank the wine, and then continued through what I was pretty sure was the entire contents of my bar. After that, things got a little hazy.

Still under the shower, I heard the bathroom door open.

"I've gotta wee," Ashliel said, poking her head in.

"Go right ahead." We'd seen each other naked dozens of times. It was nothing new and nothing to be embarrassed about.

Ashliel came in, closing the door behind her. "So. Last night."

"Yeah. I've got some blanks," I admitted, rinsing the shampoo from my hair.

"Me, too. What was in those shots?"

"I think it has more to do with how many we had."

Turning off the shower, I wrapped myself in a towel and then snatched up another to take care of my dripping hair. Ashliel sat dejectedly on the toilet, head in hands, jeans, and panties around her ankles.

"You know," she muttered, "it's Levi's fault."

I frowned. "What makes you say that?"

"You called him. And then you really hit the drink hard. Remember?"

"Um. Nope." I sighed. "Maybe that's a good thing."

"You told him what a jerk he was, and a whole lot of other things, then hung up. Not surprising, I guess since...you know."

Levi and I had been blowing hot and cold since we'd reconnected. Forgive? Sounded good. Forget? Not on your life. I was still angry over what had happened, but Levi was tenacious, and deep down, I liked that about him. It also irritated the shit out of me.

"I guess we need to get back to work," Ashliel said, her voice lacking any enthusiasm whatsoever.

"Yeah. Gotta find out what Keres meant by the rise of the witnesses. And stop Lilith from opening any more doors. Not to mention, find Keres and send her sorry ass back home."

Ashliel started across the room with her jeans and underwear still around her ankles. I stepped out of the way as she kicked them off and hopped into the shower. Before I could warn her that her top was still on, she let out a curse in the form of a howl.

I couldn't hold back my laugh.

"Lucy?" a male voice called, quickly followed by banging on my penthouse door. I hurried to answer the summons, the banging doing nothing for my headache.

"Shh." I flung open the door and leaned against the frame, eyeing Levi, who stood as fresh as a daisy before me.

"What do you want?" I grumbled. "And how did you get here? I left you on Earth."

"You asked me to come over, and Dacian gave me a lift." His eyes scoured me from top to toe, pausing over the exposed flesh of my shoulders.

"I asked you?" I lifted a brow. "When?"

"Last night. After you cussed me out, you told

me to come back today. Are you going to invite me in?" Before I could answer him, he pushed past me and made himself comfortable on a barstool at my kitchen counter.

Ashliel burst from the bathroom, towel wrapped around her body, her flaming tendrils subdued to a smolder. "Oh, you're here."

Levi waved. "Hi," he said.

Ashliel hissed, and the flames in her hair sparked and then sizzled against her wet shoulder. "Nu-uh, you don't get to say hi to me."

He frowned. "You, too?"

"Well, what did you expect? You can't be keeping secrets from your mate—especially big ass ones like there's a baby on the way. And then there's not! The truth has a way of coming out. It always does."

His face flushed the same red as the fires of Hell. "What was I supposed to do? I wanted to protect her!"

"She doesn't need your protection, Levi. She's a grown-ass woman, not to mention the Queen of Hell."

"Guys! Seriously, I'm right here." I slammed my hand against my forehead, hard. I winced at the pounding in my head.

"Hey." Levi grabbed my hands and forced them away from my face. I narrowed my eyes, trying to ignore the concern in his eyes. "It's not that bad," he assured me, rubbing his thumb across my forehead.

Sliding off the stool, I clutched my towel to my chest. "Okay, you've checked in on us, as requested. Thank you. You can go now."

"You heard her," Ashliel said. "Get out."

"It's okay, Ash." I gave her a look, telling her to stand down. I knew she had my back. To Levi, I said, "Sorry. I'm hungover; my alcohol-infused brain cannot deal with any more right now."

"But last night?" Levi frowned at me, reaching out as I backed away. Last night I'd vented, taken my anger out on him, and he'd let me. He'd listened in silence, and then, I hung up on him. Too bad I couldn't remember any of it.

My headache increased tenfold, the thumping behind my eyes almost unbearable. I could barely stay on my feet. I spun on my heel and headed for my bedroom. I was not ready to face the day after all.

CHAPTER
SEVEN

"Check this out."

We were in my office, and Ashliel was pouring over the monitors, scouring every inch of the Earth for clues as to where Keres was and where Lilith might be. I didn't know how I would stop my mother, only that it needed to be done if the Earth was to be saved. Reports were already coming in of Keres spreading disease. A new outbreak of Ebola. A new strain of deadly flu. Her arrows were toxic, and wherever they landed, illness, and death soon followed.

"You've found something?" Standing by her side, I looked at the wall of monitors as she manipulated them into the order she wanted.

"Yeah. This. A bow and arrow symbol."

"That's the seal for Keres' realm." And it was too late to stop that door from being opened — Lilith had already opened it. "We need to stop Lilith from opening more doors," I said. "Only what door would she open next? How do we get in her head?"

"Let me run this…" Ashliel's teeth gnawed on her lower lip as she concentrated on inputting data into the electronic clipboard she always carried when on the job. "There." She nodded in satisfaction. "I've run a search on other dimension symbols. If one of them is on Earth, we'll know about it." We stood in silence, watching the monitors as the search parameters she'd entered churned through data.

"He's here," Ashliel stated the obvious, for as soon as Levi stepped foot over the threshold, I felt him. After all, I'd bound him to me, my fated mate—and he had done the same. We were forever connected, and despite my being very pissed off, we had to work this out. I'd had a glimpse into my mother's mind, of the hatred and bitterness inside her, and I did not want that future for myself.

"It's okay, Ash. You can go," I told her, nodding when she eyeballed me as if I'd lost my mind. She must have decided I had, for she spun on her heel and stalked out. I couldn't help but grin. Ash was volatile, like her hair. Quick to anger and just as quick to forgive.

She passed Levi without a word, but it appeared he didn't notice—or care—he only had eyes for me. Crossing the room, he stood in front of me.

"You may have built a wall between us, but I'm going to create a door in that wall. Or find a way to climb over." His gaze drifted away as he considered his words. I bit back a grin but remained silent. Finally realizing he'd gone off into his own world and was no doubt picturing ladders and walls, he snapped his attention back to me and took both of my hands into his.

"Sometimes, we do the wrong things for the right reasons. I'm human. Correction—I was human, not all that long ago, and I'm sure I still carry a lot of my human traits."

"You carry all of your human traits Levi," I told him. For while it was true, I'd inadvertently marked him, which had subsequently turned him into a fire demon so that our two species would be compatible, he was still him. Intrinsically human.

"What I said still stands. I did the wrong thing for the right reason."

"What if I'm not ready? Did you think of that? Kids? Me? What if I'm an awful parent—an awful mother—Heaven forbid I turn out like my mom. Look at this mess. Is this my future?" I gestured to the screens, showing the turmoil Earth was currently in.

His eyes sparked with realization. "You're afraid."

"I'm not afraid of anything," I bluffed.

"It's okay to be scared, Lucy. I'm terrified—what if I fuck up my kid's life? Make the wrong choices? There isn't a parent alive who hasn't had those thoughts at least once."

"I can't believe we're standing here talking about having kids." I pulled my hands from his and turned my back, striding to the floor-to-ceiling windows and looking out over my kingdom of Hell.

"Parenthood chose us." I could feel him behind me, his warmth seeping into my bones. "We didn't ask for it. Certainly, we weren't expecting it. But it happened."

"Not quite," I whispered, my heart aching all over again. "She was taken, remember? By my father. Who lied to cover up what he'd done."

"It was an accident. He's horrified at what happened."

"Stop defending him. If what you say is true,

he'd be here explaining himself and apologizing. He's not."

"But I am." Levi spun me around to face him. "I'm sorry. I'm very, very sorry. I should have told you the minute I knew. If I could turn back the clock, do it all over, I would. But I can't. All I can do is stand here and say I'm sorry and pray you find it in your heart to forgive me."

His words touched my heart, and I knew our future was very firmly in my hands. I could accept his apology and move on, or I could hold on to my anger and hurt. I chose the former. Cupping his face in my hands, I looked into his eyes.

"I forgive you," I whispered. "But I can't forget. No more secrets, Levi. Even if you think it's something I don't want to hear or something that will hurt me."

Without hesitation, he nodded. "I promise. Never again."

"And the whole kid thing? I'm not sure I'm ready. Can we shelve that topic until this mess with my mom is cleaned up?"

"Absolutely. There's no rush. I didn't plan it either, Lucy, but let me be honest and say that when I knew you were pregnant, I was the happiest man alive."

I blinked, unsure of how to react. "Oh."

"I'm still the happiest man alive," he added hurriedly. "Baby or no baby. But you're right. Bringing a child into the world when the Apocalypse is upon us isn't the smartest move."

"Right. We've got several problems." I headed back to the wall of monitors and stood, hands-on-hips, watching the live feeds.

"Your mom. Keres. And...there's more?" Levi guessed.

"Yes. Mom is opening doors to other dimensions. Keres said it was the calling of the witnesses. We don't know what that means. If we can work it out, maybe we'll be able to work out what door is next and stop her."

"How do we stop her? And how do we stop Keres?"

"With help."

"Dacian." Levi cracked his knuckles and rotated his neck, ready for a fight.

"And his Army of Angels. And trust me, we're going to need an army." Lilith was smart and determined. Plus, she had been planning this for a long time. If we couldn't outsmart her, we'd have to take her by force.

"And your dad?"

"Dacian can liaise with him." I wasn't prepared to face my father, not yet. I was making progress with my forgiveness of Levi, but my dad was another matter. My daughter was now a part of his essence; I couldn't stand to be near him.

"Ashliel," I called for my second in command, and she appeared in the doorway instantly.

"Yes?"

"Get Dacian here. Apprise him of the situation, although I'm sure he's aware Keres is loose on Earth. We need to work together on this one. Oh, and I'm going to check in on the key."

"You think it's at risk?" She quirked a dark brow, her eyes drilling into mine with such intensity that I blinked.

"Lilith knows about them, for she triggered their tattoos. I need to go and ward them, hide the Island if I can. Plus, I left Nibbler there. I miss the fuzzy butt."

"Nibbler?" Levi asked.

"The cutest orange kitten you've ever seen," I explained, clasping his hand in mine. The jolt of our palms connecting was powerful, electricity shooting up my arm. "We need to go back to Fury Island and check on them. I wouldn't put it past Lilith to try and take them, use them as leverage against me."

Keeping a firm hold on Levi, I flew us to Fury Island, landing outside the cottage where I'd been staying when I first fled Heaven. Everything was exactly as I'd left it, and I breathed a sigh of relief.

"Lucy!" The front door opened, and Del stood there, Nibbler cradled against her chest, and Duke squeezed at her side.

"Hey, Del. Thanks for taking care of her." I reached out and took Nibbler from her, scratching the little bundle under the ear and being rewarded with her loud purr. "I've missed you, baby," I whispered, burying my face in her fur.

"She missed you, too. She never purrs that loudly for me." Del smiled, then stood back, ushering us into the cottage. "Tell me what's been happening. What was that tsunami all about? And I've seen on the news all the outbreaks of illness—is that Lilith, too?"

"The illness is Keres, a death spirit. Lilith is opening doors to other dimensions in something that's called the calling of the witnesses."

Del shook her head. "This is madness." Turning her attention to Levi, she held out her hand. "We didn't get properly introduced last time, what with a tsunami barreling down on us. I'm Del, and this is Duke."

Levi shook her hand and smiled. "Levi, pleased to meet you. So, where's the third part of the key? Jase, isn't it?"

"He's at work. He's a vet. I figured I'd wait here for Lucy to come back, keep Nibbler company."

"Sorry I didn't return straight away," I said, sinking down into the sofa. I rested my head on the back and stared up at the ceiling. So many nights, I'd sat in this exact same spot and looked at the exact same ceiling. Nibbler snuggled in under my chin, her purr vibrating through me. It was comforting.

"Great to meet you, Levi. I'll leave you guys to it. Are you staying a while, Lucy?" Del snapped her fingers, and Duke sprang up from where he'd been laying at my feet.

"We need to get back to Hell," I said, a wave of sadness washing over me. I liked it here; I'd be sorry to leave.

Hearing the sadness in my tone, Levi squeezed my shoulder. "Surely we can stay awhile? Ashliel can call if anything comes up."

I smiled. "Okay, maybe a couple of hours."

Del beamed at us. "Fantastic. Let me know if you need me to take Nibbler for you when you go back."

At the thought of leaving Nibbler behind, I pulled the tiny kitten closer to me, making her meow in protest. Loosening my grip, I kissed her head. "I'm not leaving her. She'll come with me. But thank you, Del."

Levi saw Del out, then returned to sit next to me on the sofa. "So, what's next?"

I blew out a breath, "Honestly? I don't know. This is such a mess. Everything is happening so fast I don't know which way to turn. All I want to do right this second is sit here and cuddle this kitten."

Levi's face softened as he scratched Nibbler under the chin. "Then that's what we'll do." Silence descended, and it was blissful. Eventually, Levi murmured, "I wonder what Mr. Meow will think of Nibbler? I think he'd like to have a little sister." Mr. Meow was Levi's cat, and we hadn't been able to bring ourselves to re-home him—he now resided in Hell HQ with us. The ache in my chest had finally gone, thanks to the man by my side and the two fur babies that were now an intrinsic part of our lives.

CHAPTER
EIGHT

"Lucy. Levi." Dacian stood before us, blue eyes sparkling. He looked good. His new role as God's right-hand man suited him.

"Thanks for coming. You know about Keres?" I asked.

Dacian inclined his head. "We do."

"I suggest we join forces to sort this mess out. I'm pretty sure it's Lilith opening the doors." I took a seat at my desk. Following my lead, Levi sat in the chair opposite me while Dacian took the other.

"Agreed. It seems logical now that your father has been found that she's putting her plan into fruition."

"Is that why she waited, do you think? She's had

thousands of years to destroy the Earth if she wanted to. Why wait until now?"

Dacian rubbed at the back of his neck. "Well, it's no fun if your dad isn't around to see her do it. Her ultimate goal is to bring him pain. Destroying his creations is a sure-fire way to do that."

"And yet Dad isn't here? Doesn't he want to stop her?" I probed, concerned that my father still hadn't put in an appearance.

"Your father is..." Dacian paused, considering his words.

"What?" I snapped. "He's what? Too busy?"

"Weak. He's too weak. He pushed himself hard repairing the damage and neglect your brothers inflicted on Heaven."

I sat in stunned silence. Dad had almost killed me when he drained my magic to save himself. The last time I'd seen him, he'd looked good. Fully restored and strong. To hear that wasn't the case was a shock. And as much as I hated it, it made sense that Heaven needed his attention first—it was his realm after all. Earth and Hell would have to wait.

"If Lilith knew this..." Levi looked from Dacian to me and back again.

"There is a lot Lilith doesn't know, and we need to keep it that way," Dacian said, a new air of authority ringing in his voice.

I smiled. Now that he was no longer under the control of my brothers, Michael and Gabriel, Dacian was doing what he did best. He was a warrior. A soldier. He had this and was confident we'd bring Lilith down and stop the Apocalypse.

"What's the plan?" I asked, leaning back and steepling my fingers beneath my chin.

He held up two fingers. "We have two objectives, one, stop Keres. Two, stop Lilith."

"Sounds easy," Levi joked, rolling his eyes. "How do we do either of those things?"

"Two teams. One goes after Lilith. The other clean up the mess she unleashes." He turned his gaze toward the wall of screens. "I can see by your monitors that finding Keres will be relatively easy; she's leaving a path of destruction. But Lilith? We can't pick her up on any of our scans—can you?"

I shook my head. "No sign of her so far. I figured she wasn't on Earth. You think she is?"

Dacian was already nodding. "The doors being opened are on Earth. She has to be there. The quicker she opens the doors, the sooner the

Apocalypse starts. She's not going to waste time. She's there, but she's cloaked somehow."

"Do you know what calling of the witnesses means?" Levi asked.

Dacian frowned as he stared out the window. Finally, he said, "It's old. It's something like a court for the Gods. I'd have to go through the archives."

"God's law?" Levi asked, confused.

Dacian shook his head and then turned to me. "Not your father's law," he clarified. "It's the law to Gods and Goddesses across all the realms, all the universes."

"But who would control that? Who would be responsible?" It seemed an incredible responsibility, and I balked at the sheer magnitude of it.

"I can't recall the details." Dacian shrugged. "As I said, I'll have to visit the archives. Why?"

"Because Keres told us Lilith is calling the witnesses. We need to know what that means."

Dacian's nose wrinkled as he shook his head. "Nothing good."

I rubbed my temples and called out, "Ashliel!"

She appeared immediately. "Here," she said, crossing the room to stand by my desk. "What do you need?"

"Dacian, can you work with Ashliel on the

witness's angle? She may be able to dig up something we can work with from here. Levi and I will go after Keres. I'll take three of my best demons—I assume you have your angels, Dacian? If not, take whoever you need. Except for Ashliel. She stays here."

Dacian rose, and I caught the look of appreciation in his eyes before he raised a hand to guard them. I was pretty sure he had the hots for Ashliel. And judging by the flush in her cheeks, I figured she felt the same. I bit back a grin as the two of them darted awkward yet endearing glances at each other.

"What do you need to know?" Ashliel asked him.

He touched a hand to the small of her back and guided her away from us. As they walked, he said, "We need to know the laws of the witnesses. Lilith is calling the witnesses; we need to know exactly what that means. And how to stop her."

"Ooh, this is gonna be fun!" Ashliel's voice was full of enthusiasm, and she began talking and flicking through her electronic clipboard.

I waited until they'd left before turning my attention to Levi. "Are you ready for this?" I asked. "Bringing down Keres will not be easy."

He winked at me. "I was born ready."

I barked out a laugh. "No, you weren't. You were born a human psychic. I bet you didn't see this coming."

He laughed with me. "Actually, you're right. This is far from what I ever envisaged my life being. But…"

My smile slipped, and he held up a hand. "No regrets. I wouldn't trade this…" Lowering his hand, he waved it around at our surroundings. "…Or you, for anything."

I studied him for a moment before letting it drop. What was done was done. I hadn't meant to mark him, turn him into a Fire Demon, but I had, and there was no turning back.

"So, how do we bring this death spirit down?" Levi asked, bringing my attention back to the matter at hand.

"Ashliel sent me through some info on that. She's been doing some research on Keres. Initially, I thought I'd have to kill her, but if I use her weapon against her, I can send her back to her own realm and close the door."

Levi flinched. "What, steal her bow and arrow?"

I nodded. "We have to pierce her flesh with her own arrow."

He cocked his head. "How do we get her arrow?"

"They were flying thick and fast in the alley." I shrugged. "I say we go pick one up." I rubbed at my shoulder where one of her arrows had found its mark, remembering the pain.

After using my magic to send my demons to Earth, I took Levi's hand and flew us to the alley. There was not an arrow in sight.

"I don't get it." Running a hand around the back of his neck, Levi scoured the alley, but it was useless. There weren't any arrows here. "Where did they go?"

"Maybe some humans picked them up? Or Keres retrieved them." It was a guess, but it didn't matter what had happened to them. The only thing that did matter was we didn't have one to use against Keres. That meant that I had to engage her in battle again. I whistled, drawing the attention of the three demons who were investigating the alley behind Levi. They immediately stopped and looked at me, waiting for their orders.

"I'm going to contact Ashliel, get Keres' location. We will engage her in battle. Be ready. Have your weapons in hand; she is fast. To send her back to her own dimension, you need to use her own weapon against her, which means get your hands on an arrow and stab her with it. You don't have to kill her. Just breaking the skin should do it. It sounds easy, but it won't be. Keres will know this is a vulnerability; she will guard against it. I suspect that is why there are no arrows left behind."

"The arrows are magic, then?" Levi asked.

"Probably have some spell on them that will return them to her if they don't hit their target. We could spend time trying to find out that spell and break it."

"That would take time we don't have." Levi sighed. "Have you heard the latest? A plague outbreak. We haven't had the plague on Earth for years, and now there is an outbreak in every country —she sure gets around."

I nodded. "And it's a great distraction technique."

"Oh?"

"Keep the humans busy with trying to contain the sickness. The governments and military are all focused on this. Then another door opens, and another fresh Hell is unleashed on Earth."

"This could get...nuclear," he said in a grim voice.

"Exactly. We need to know who these witnesses are. Who is she going to call next?"

"How?"

"I've got no idea. I'm trusting Ashliel and Dacian can gather more intel for us."

"Okay. We don't have time to work out Keres's spell on her arrows, then. But they carry disease. Are we vulnerable to them?"

"My magic cleared the toxins from my system pretty quickly—I suspect it would be the same for my demons, but you? You carry human DNA. You need to either suit up or stay out of this one."

"I'll suit up. There's no way I'm sitting this out."

"I knew you'd say that." With a wave of my hand, I coated Levi in black armor, and while it looked like metal, it was as flexible as any fabric.

"Neat." He grinned at me, arms spread out, admiring his outfit. "I look like a ninja."

"You need to move like one, too, if you don't want to get hit!"

I looked at the three demons, who were still waiting patiently for my orders. "Ready?"

"Affirmative," they said in unison, their wings spanning the width of the alley.

I utilized the connection I had to Ashliel,

regardless of what realm I was in. "Ashliel? I need an updated location on Keres."

"She's in Australia. Tasmania, to be precise. The city of Launceston."

"Got it. Thanks, Ash."

Spreading my wings, I motioned Levi to my side, for while he was a human fire demon hybrid, he couldn't fly. He crossed to my side and slid an arm around my waist, and I did the same. "Ready?" I asked.

"Let's do it," he replied, and with one big whoosh of my wings, we were airborne, my demons following close behind. Traveling at inhuman speeds, it took us mere seconds to arrive at Launceston. Even from a distance, I could see the green cloud encasing the city. "Cover your nose and mouth," I said to Levi as we approached. "I don't want you breathing any of that in." Glancing at my demons, I yelled, "Ready?"

"Affirmative," they roared back, nearly in sync.

"Attack on sight," I instructed, and they immediately darted in front of me, zigzagging and weaving over and around each other as we approached. Levi tugged the fabric of his armor over his nose and mouth and then clutched his sword, his knuckles white.

I caught sight of Keres, already engaged in battle with the demons up ahead. I came in to land, releasing Levi and drawing my sword. I'd deliberately set Levi down a little farther away than necessary, and he growled his displeasure at me as I flew on ahead.

"You've been busy," I shouted at Keres over the din of battle. Her arrows flew as fast as any bullets, but my demons deflected them with spears and swords. Unfortunately, their strikes had little effect.

"You took your time," she yelled back. "I've achieved a lot in your absence. See this mist? Every breath they take, they suck mutant spores into their lungs, like acid, it will eat away at them. Every man, woman, and child will be destroyed from the inside out."

"Bitch," I hissed through clenched teeth. She was goading me. Her gaze darted to Levi, and I knew she was aware of Levi's weakness. He was part human. And I guessed Lilith had filled her in on our relationship because while Levi's humanity was seen as a weakness, Levi himself was *my* weakness.

They could use him against me.

I wouldn't let that happen.

I swooped in low and fast, slashing my sword, catching Keres on the forearm. Blood exploded into the air before the wound healed itself. I joined my demons in dive-bombing the death spirit, swooping low then high, coming in at different angles, all the while keeping an eye on Levi, who was fast approaching on foot. I needed him to remember to grab an arrow but didn't want to yell it out in front of Keres, given it might tip her off about our intentions.

An arrow caught one of my demons' wings and sent him spinning out of control. He crashed into the ground. Precious seconds were lost as he wrenched the arrow from the membrane of his wing, healed himself, and went back into battle.

Only, he hadn't kept hold of the arrow; he'd thrown it to the ground in anger. *Damn it.* I shot him an angry look, but his focus was on Keres.

Levi spotted the arrow and veered toward it. The arrow didn't return to Keres because it found its target. It hit the demon. As Keres's head turned in Levi's direction, I realized this might be our only shot. I quickly flew in front, blocking her view, while behind me, Levi's hand scraped the pavement as he snatched up the arrow. Every fiber of my being wanted to take the arrow from Levi and finish the job, but I knew that would be a mistake. We had to use Levi to our advantage. Keres didn't consider him a threat because of his human DNA, and as such, barely paid him any attention.

It worked.

The demon who had been hit was attacking with renewed fervor, furious he'd been injured and taking his wrath out with a rapid-fire attack. I joined in along with the other two demons.

As Levi drew closer, I kept myself between him and Keres, giving him extra protection while affording him the opportunity to get close enough to attack. I didn't expect what happened next, and I swear my heart stopped in my chest.

Levi vaulted onto Keres's back, wrapped one arm around her neck, and with the other, plunged the arrow into her side. Keres bellowed, dislodging the arrow as Levi leaped clear.

Then, she vanished.

Poof. Gone.

My heart resumed beating, and I turned to Levi in relief.

"You did it!" I grinned, wiping sweat from my brow. It had been a fast-paced fight, and I was winded, as were my demons, judging from the puffing coming from behind me as they landed.

"Fuck, that was epic!" Levi beamed, clearly pleased with himself. Hell, I was pleased with him, too. He'd remained focused and had done what needed to be done.

"Look." One of the demons pointed, and I looked up to see the green mist clear. Keres had been sent back to her dimension, and with her, all of her disease.

"We failed." Dacian's voice was as grim as his face.

"Another door opened?" I asked.

He nodded.

"Then we work on stopping her from opening a third. Do we know who she called?" Planting my hands on my hips, I waited.

"Not yet. Just a shift in the Earth's energy indicating a dimension breach. You had success, though? Keres has been banished?"

"She has. Thanks to Levi. You taught him well." I slapped Dacian on the shoulder since he was the one that trained Levi.

"So now we have another creature to take

down?" Levi asked, rubbing his hands together, looking like he was keen for the battle.

"We do," I said. "But, we need to know what we're dealing with first."

"Can't we use their weapon against them? Like we did with the death spirit?"

"That'd be too easy," I sighed, rubbing my hand around the back of my neck. I was tired and sweaty.

"I'm going to take a shower," I told them. "I need to clear my head. Dacian, you've updated Ashliel?"

"Yeah, she's still working on the witness angle as well as nailing down this latest threat," Dacian said. "I'm going to check Heaven's archives; this is taking longer than I expected. And let me know when you've got a hit on the latest threat."

"Will do." To Levi, I said, "Get some rest. We need to get back out there and send whoever Lilith let in back to their own dimension."

"But we don't know how," he protested.

"We'll find out. We always do."

IT CAME to me standing beneath the spray of the shower. As I closed my eyes and tipped my head back, the water flowed over my face, and I heard it. Dad's voice. The power of three.

My eyes flew open, and I blinked, glancing around in shock. Was Dad here? In my bathroom? Slapping one hand across my breasts and the other across my lady bits, I squinted through the steam. "Dad?"

No reply.

Stepping out from the shower, I grabbed a towel and wrapped myself in it, but still no sign of Dad. But, he'd sent me a message from inside the condensation, for on the mirror were the exact words he'd spoken.

The power of three.

The door flew open, and Levi was there, bare-chested, shirt clutched in one hand.

"You alright? Thought I heard you call out?" His gaze scanned the room before coming to rest on me, and I felt the heat of his gaze all the way to my toes. It had been a while since we'd been intimate, and my body was reminding me of that fact.

"I'm fine." I couldn't contain the hitch in my throat.

"You need to stop looking at me like that if you don't want me to follow through," he growled, his eyes darkening.

"Who says I don't want you to follow through?" I challenged. It was all he needed. With lightning speed, he pressed me up against the tile, one hand slipping behind my neck, his mouth coming down on mine.

"I missed this," I breathed, breaking the kiss. "I missed your kiss, your taste, your touch." Frantically, I wound my arms around his neck and pulled him close for another kiss, wanting more, wanting everything he could give me. His growl vibrated through me, setting my nerve endings on fire, as did his fingers that trailed down my side, taking my towel with them. I stood naked, trembling, and pressed against him.

He lifted his head, and I mewled in protest. Dark desire flashed in his eyes. He wanted me as much as I wanted him. Loved me as much as I loved him. Despite what had happened, we were back together, as we were meant to be.

"Jesus, Lucy," he groaned. "Stop looking at me like that."

"Like what?" I breathed.

"Like you want to fuck me every which way there is, and then do it all over again."

"But I do," I whispered, dropping kisses on his

chest. "That's exactly what I want to do." A squeal escaped as he pulled us into the still running shower. Water cascaded over us, and I laughed. "You still have your pants on."

"Don't care."

I loved this side of him, this raw, primal, alpha male side. It excited me even more. He smelled so good, like a heady aphrodisiac. Every nerve in my body was aching for his touch. A whimper escaped my mouth as I pulled him closer, the muscles on his back taut under my hands.

"You feel so good," I groaned into his mouth.

He chuckled. "Took the words right out of my mouth, babe."

It was time to banish the pain that existed between us, the hurt of what had transpired the last time we were together like this. I bit his lip, tasted blood, and didn't care. He returned the favor, sensing that I didn't want gentle. I wanted unbridled passion; I wanted out of control lust.

The aftermath was bittersweet. My body was sated, my heart was whole, yet there was a tiny piece that was empty. A silent tear tracked down my cheek. Levi studied my face, then wiped the tear away with his thumb.

"I love you," he whispered, his voice raw with emotion.

I nodded. "I know." After taking in a deep breath, I added something else that I knew. "I'm sorry," I whispered back. "It wasn't your fault. I love you, too."

"What do you think it means?" Levi murmured.

We were lying in bed, wrapped in each other's arms, and I didn't have to ask what he was talking about. We were that in sync.

"I don't know," I replied. "But it was Dad's voice I heard. That he delivered the message twice in two different mediums means he really wanted me to receive it." I ignored the twinge of hurt that my father hadn't delivered the message in person. Sure, Dacian had said he was weak, but I knew the real reason he avoided me. For good reason, because I was still pissed as Hell about what he'd done.

"The power of three." He absently ran his hand

up and down my spine while I lay curled against his chest, my fingers dancing across his skin.

"I've got it!" He sat up, dislodging me. I grumbled in protest. "He has three children! It's you, Michael, and Gabriel! Has to be!" His voice rose three octaves in excitement.

I sat up, wrapping my arms around my knees as I considered it. He could be right. What other three could there be? Me and my brothers were powerful archangels, and for the last millennia, we'd been divided. What if, together, the three of us were more powerful than we realized? Powerful enough to stop Lilith, to stop the calling of the witnesses?

"We have to find them." Swinging my legs out of bed, I stood, feeling the heat of Levi's gaze on my naked back. I smiled at him over my shoulder and asked, "You still want more?"

"I can never get enough of you," he declared, climbing off the bed and coming to stand in front of me. Tracing the line of my jaw with one finger, he made me shiver.

"I like this side of you," I breathed. "Insatiable."

"I've always been insatiable when it comes to you."

"We need to find my brothers," I reminded him,

crossing to my dressing room and eyeballing the outfits lined up neatly on hangers.

"Your dad banished them to Earth. To live as humans," Levi said as if I needed reminding.

I played with the belt of my robe, considering. "Maybe he's lifted their punishment? After all, he sent me the message."

"Yeah, but if he's given them back their angelic powers, do you think they'd hang around on Earth? They could be anywhere."

"True. But we'll find them."

Mr. Meow appeared, rubbing around my ankles and purring. "Hey, buddy, where have you been, hm? Want some dinner?" The cat meowed and bumped his forehead against my shin, making me laugh. Nibbler came running out, chasing Mr. Meow's tail.

"Levi, take care of your cat! I'm taking a shower. Alone."

My shower was fast, and as I was drying myself, Levi cooed to the cats while he prepared their food. I grinned at the fact such a small creature could bring a grown man to his knees.

I was still chuckling over Levi when Ashliel hissed, "Lucy," into my ear.

"On my way." Dressed in red jeans, a white

sequined top, stiletto heels, and sporting a messy bun on the top of my head, I summoned the elevator to take me to my office.

"What have you got?" I asked, striding across the vast expanse of my office to where Ashliel stood in front of the monitor bank. She pointed at a news report, and I watched, brows knitted together in a frown. Images on the screens stuttered, but all the news reports were the same. Unprecedented acts of war and hostility were breaking out all over the globe.

"Only one thing can do that," Ashliel told me.

"A Valkyrie," I said.

She turned toward me. "This could go nuclear."

"I won't let that happen," I assured her, although, at this point, I wasn't sure how I was going to stop the Valkyrie.

"Do you have any leads on Gabriel and Michael?" I asked Ashliel, moving from the monitors to look out the massive windows that afforded me the best view of Hell. I leaned one hand against the glass and looked down at my kingdom, the demons patrolling the skies, keeping our realm safe, the hustle and bustle of life on the streets below. People thought of Hell as one massive ball of fire, but it wasn't that at all. It was so much more. Sure, we had holding cells that went on for miles where sinners arrived to atone for their sins. And we had the pit, where the evilest of souls would burn for all eternity, but the rest of Hell was beautiful. The skies were perpetual pinks, purples, and oranges that created an everlasting twilight. There were beaches, and although you wouldn't want to swim in the acidic ocean, the sight was unmatched in all the realms. We had mountains—although it would take you a lifetime to reach them.

"Nothing," Ashliel said, dragging my attention back to her. "Why are you even worried about those assholes anyway? They've been nothing but trouble for you. Why give them any loyalty? They sure don't deserve it."

"Send a message to Heaven asking for a report on their status. Or ask Dacian directly. I don't care. I want answers. Dad sent me a message."

"Oh?" That got her attention, and her head snapped around so fast I winced.

"The power of three," I told her.

She screwed her mouth up, mulling over the words. I could practically see the cogs turning in her head. Ashliel was a veritable database; I'd be lost without her. "And you think he was referring to you and your brothers? That the three of you combined..." she trailed off, tapping a fingernail against her lip, eyes unseeing as she disappeared into deep thought.

"Gabriel and Michael were stripped of their angelic powers and banished to Earth to live as humans—as punishment for their actions—or lack of action, in running Heaven." The pacing began, as it always did when she was unraveling a puzzle. I settled on the sofa and waited in silence.

"Lilith is calling the witnesses, opening doors to other dimensions, intending—we assume—to start the Apocalypse and destroy every living creature on Earth. She's the one who told you what your dad had done to you...in the hopes of getting you on her side. Again, that's an assumption, but I'd say it's accurate." She nodded to herself, talking out loud. I remained silent; she didn't need my input. "She's probably letting your anger at your father fester for a bit before approaching you. So, in the meantime, if I were her, I'd recruit your brothers—her sons. She could return their powers, and given your brother's personalities, I'd say they'd join forces with her without hesitation. After all, they tried to destroy Earth themselves. Being rid of it once and for all would be very appealing to them." She stopped pacing, took in a deep breath, and then went on.

"But why does she need them? Is it purely motherly love that she wants you all by her side? After all, the creatures she's inviting to Earth can destroy it; she doesn't need Michael and Gabriel for that."

"She wants more than Earth," I said.

She looked at me, her eyes narrowing.

"Hell will be next," she predicted, and a shiver danced over my skin at the surety in her words. "Hell is God's creation, and she's out to destroy every last piece of him. She'll need your brothers for that. She'll need you."

"The power of three," I said, breathless.

Ashliel nodded. "Your dad sent a warning."

"She's assuming I will side with her, though. And I won't. No matter what my father has done, he doesn't deserve this. She imprisoned him for thousands of years, left him to rot. And in punishing him, she punished me, for like it or not, I love my dad." I felt tears gather in my eyes and blinked to dispel them.

"We have to protect him," I whispered, for Dacian's words came back to me. He was weak. He'd used precious energy to restore Heaven. He needed time to regroup. If Lilith realized he was vulnerable, she would strike now, take Heaven, and if she had my brothers with her, she just might pull it off.

"Do not breathe a word of this," I ordered, striding to my desk. "This information cannot leak."

"You think we have a leak?" She sounded surprised, but I shook my head. "No. I don't. But if I was Lilith and I had plans as big as hers, I'd be planting spies, for while I was busy with plan a—calling the witnesses—I'd be wanting intel on the next stage, learn Hell's weaknesses."

"The key," we said in unison.

ELEVEN

We were back on Fury Island. Even though I'd warded the island and the vessels containing the key to the gates of Hell, I had an uneasy feeling that Del, Jase, and Duke were in danger.

I could feel the connection I had with them, stronger now that I was close. It was like a rubber band stretched between us, pulling me toward them. And they'd feel it, too, would know I was nearby.

"I wish you could feel what I'm feeling," I said to Levi, clasping a hand over my chest. "It's the weirdest thing."

Levi was glancing around with narrow eyes as he squeezed my hand tight. "Something is off."

"Are you sure?" I frowned. "I don't feel it."

"I think your bond with the key is overpowering your other senses," he muttered, dragging me down the dock and onto the sidewalk that ran the entire length of the shore. Shops were squeezed in side by side, catering to the tourist crowd. Only...there was no tourist crowd. The sidewalks were empty. Even the birds had stopped flying overhead.

We hurried along, peering into each shop as we went. It was as if everyone had simply vanished. Coffee cups sat half-finished. Lights were on, doors unlocked, yet not a single soul was to be seen.

"Did Keres reach here before we stopped her?" Levi pondered.

I shook my head. "One of her arrows could have easily taken out the island's population. But this quickly? And if that were the case, where are the bodies?"

"I can feel the key, though. They're still alive." But aside from that connection, there was a rising sense of panic. Where were the townsfolk of Fury Island? What had happened here? Something supernatural, I was sure of it.

Kicking at the pavement, I spun and paced. "So many unanswered questions. I'm getting a damn headache."

"We should grab the key and get out of here." He clenched his jaw. "This is a trap."

"You think so?" That was one possibility I hadn't considered. I pinched the bridge of my nose and closed my eyes. I really did have a headache, and there was a buzzing in my ears that was growing louder and more irritating by the second. "Do you hear that?"

"What?"

"A buzzing. A really irritating, loud, buzzing."

"I don't hear anything other than the ocean." Levi frowned at me and then looked around again, clearly on edge. "We should have brought backup. Or Dacian. Or both."

"I can handle this," I protested, stung that he thought I needed help. We were here to retrieve Del, Jase, and Duke, to bring them to Hell for safekeeping while all the madness was going on.

"I know you can. That wasn't what I meant. I just have a bad feeling about this. A really bad feeling."

I tilted my head and studied his expression, trying to read the lines of his face. "A psychic one?"

"Sort of. Not a vision. Not a message. But a sixth sense that something bad is about to go down. Something awful."

"Let's get them and get out of here." Spinning on my heel, I backtracked to the end of the block and headed inland. I knew the way to the Vet's house like the back of my hand, only the closer I got, the louder the buzzing in my head roared. Soon, it was so loud that my teeth were chattering, and my eyeballs were in danger of popping clean out of my head.

"Argh." I collapsed to my knees, pressing the heels of my hands against my temples.

"Lucy?" Levi crouched next to me, concern pouring out of him in waves.

"Head," I groaned. "Explode." The pain was so severe that I could barely speak.

"You're bleeding. Fuck!" He ran his thumb across my upper lip, then pulled his hand back, revealing a smear of blood.

"You need to get out of here. Now," Levi shouted, scooping me up into his arms. He ran back toward the foreshore. Each step he took lessened the buzzing until we were back on the dock, and it was nothing but a faint hum. That didn't stop my brain from feeling like it had melted and was in the process of oozing out of my nose.

Laying me on the dock, he leaned over, brushing my hair from my face.

"We've got to get you out of here," he murmured, "Can you fly?"

"We can't leave the key," I protested. "And how did you know to bring me back here? And why aren't you affected?"

"Typical, full of fucking questions. You didn't hear the noise until we were off the dock. The farther inland we went, the worse it got. Therefore, it made sense to come back here. It was a guess."

"A lucky one," I muttered, flinging an arm across my eyes to block the overhead sun that was burning out my retinas.

"As for why I can't hear it? I don't know. Maybe it was targeted specifically at you."

"Which means..."

"Your brothers or your mother," he supplied. "And they knew you were coming. Which means I was right. It's a trap."

"We do not have a spy in Hell," I grumbled, refusing to consider such a thing. "We simply do not. My people are loyal." Nausea churned in my stomach, and sweat broke over my skin.

"We need to leave." His tone was more urgent. He laid the back of his hand against my forehead and frowned.

"I'm not leaving without the key." I set my jaw.

There was no way I'd leave Del, Jase, and Duke for Lilith. But what Levi said was true. Someone had gotten past the wards I'd cast, set a trap here, someone had known I was coming, and as soon as I'd stepped off the dock, it had been triggered. I crawled to the edge of the dock to vomit out the contents of my stomach, worry consuming me.

"I'll go get them and bring them to you. This trap was laid for you, not me. You wait here. I'll be back soon."

I didn't protest, wanting to focus on regaining my energy while he retrieved the key.

CHAPTER
TWELVE

The humming in my head was completely gone, and I was feeling marginally better by the time Levi returned.

Empty-handed. I pushed to my feet so fast, he doubled back.

"Where is the key?" I demanded. "Levi!" I limped forward, my eyes wide with panic. "Where are they?"

He held his hands up. "I couldn't find them. I couldn't find anyone. This place is deserted. I've been running around all over and found nothing. There's no one."

My nostrils flared in irritation even though I knew it wasn't his fault. It was stupid of me to send him off searching for the key when he had no way of tracking them.

"I'm feeling better. I'll get them myself." I headed back down the dock, gaze darting from side to side, waiting for the humming to return, but it remained blessedly absent. Even as I stepped off the dock and onto the sidewalk, nothing. Levi was right behind me, ranting that we had to leave, that it wasn't safe for me. I ignored him. The key was important, and I wasn't leaving the island without it.

"Wait here," I told him, extending my wings and flying over the town, up the hill to where their energy pooled. I had a direct line to them. All I had to do was zoom in, carry them down to the dock, retrieve Levi, and we were out of there. I ignored the blood dripping from my nose and the fact that my vision was slightly blurred.

I landed outside Del's cottage on the hillside and sucked in a deep breath. All three of them were here. I could sense them. Opening the door, I stepped inside, and sure enough, they were huddled against the far wall behind a woman I'd never seen before. Dressed in a skin-tight silver camouflage catsuit, her hair was pulled tight in a high ponytail while white stripes were painted across her cheeks and forehead.

I scanned her up and down, taking in the weapons strapped to her legs and across her back. Unable to help it, I smiled. She was badass, a war spirit, a Valkyrie.

My gaze met Jase's, who was standing protectively in front of Del, the fingers of one hand keeping a firm grasp on Duke's collar to keep him from lunging at the woman who had them trapped. I could see their marks glowing, identifying them. Could the Valkyrie see the marks, too?

"Finally. I thought you were never going to get here," the Valkyrie drawled, inching closer to me.

"Why? Why wait for me? Why the trap?" I stood with my arms by my side, relaxed yet on the alert. She hadn't drawn a weapon, but she didn't need one. She could turn me against everyone and everything, and there was no use pretending I didn't know that.

"You have something we need." She stood with legs braced, hands-on-hips. Power and authority rolled off her, and I could picture her as a great general from wars past.

"We?" I asked, although I already knew. From the smirk that curled her lips, she knew I was stalling.

"Lilith." Something like hunger danced in her eyes. "Your mother."

Del gasped, but I kept my attention on the Valkyrie. "What is it you want from me?"

"Your sword."

I blinked. Her response surprised me. I hadn't expected her to want my sword, of all things. "What does she need my sword for?" It tingled from its hiding place between my wings, eager for action. Still, I hesitated, not wanting to reveal the one thing she was after.

"It is the sword of souls. Together with the sword of angels, she can..." She stopped abruptly, clamping her lips together as if she'd revealed too much.

"She can what?" I snapped, taking a step closer.

She stiffened, and one hand moved to a pistol secured in a holster on her thigh. Bullets couldn't kill me. They hurt for a moment, sure, but they wouldn't slow me down much. Unless, of course, the bullets were spelled. That would be a different story altogether and one best avoided. Slowly, I began inching toward Del and Jase, keeping myself between them and the Valkyrie. She allowed it, swiveling her body to keep me in her line of sight. It was true then. She wasn't after the key. But their identity was compromised, and I needed to get them out of here, back to Hell where they'd be safe.

She sniggered. "I told you, I'm not here for them." She waved an arm at the door. "Go. You can all go. You included Lucifer...once you hand over your sword."

I glanced at Jase over my shoulder and gave him a slight nod. I'd accept the Valkyrie's word that she would let them go, and the sooner they were out of the house, the better. A battle was about to go down because I had no intention of handing over my sword.

"Go to the dock," I whispered under my breath as they passed me. The Valkyrie and I kept our gazes locked on each other as the trio tiptoed past. We didn't blink until the front door clicked shut behind them. I sagged, releasing a breath I didn't know I'd been holding. They were safe.

For now.

The next thing I knew, I was looking down the barrel of a gun. I hadn't seen her move. Just like Keres, she had lighting fast reflexes.

"Hand it over," she demanded, motioning with the gun.

Slowly, I moved my arm up, reaching over my head to wrap my fingers securely around the hilt of my sword. She'd get it all right, right between her ribs. With one smooth motion, I unleashed the sword and sliced through the air, missing her wrist by a hairsbreadth. Her finger pulled the trigger, and a bullet shot out of the barrel.

It was my turn to be fast, faster than I'd been against Keres and her arrows. I deflected shot after shot with the sword. Its blade, made from the ashes of Hell, shimmered with my flame. Bullets ricocheted and embedded themselves into the walls and furniture.

Then, the humming in my head started again, the buzzing louder. I had to stop this now, for if I lost concentration and fell, the sword would be hers, and for whatever reason my mother wanted it, I couldn't let it fall into her hands. Outside there was a commotion, shouting, a scream. I wanted to turn my head, to glance out the window, but didn't take my eyes from the Valkyrie who was approaching, pistol aimed at my head.

The warm wetness of blood trickled over my lips. My nose was bleeding, probably caused by the infernal buzzing scrambling my brain. I planted my feet and focused my thoughts on ending the fight.

With a mighty swing, I made contact, severing her hand. The pistol, with her fingers still clutched around it, fell to the floor. I wanted to enjoy the look of surprise on her face, then her scream as she clutched her stump and tried frantically to stem the bleeding, but time wasn't on my side. I needed to send this asshole back to her own dimension. After another spin and kick, she crashed to the floor, landing on her back. I stood over her, my blood dripping down. Raising my sword, I brought it down hard into her chest, piercing her heart. She vanished, her startled cry echoing into nothing.

The buzzing didn't stop, though. Dropping to my knees, I hid my sword back between my wings and clutched my head in my hands. The Valkyrie didn't set this trap; she wasn't doing this to me. It was Lilith. And I knew why. She wanted both. The key and the sword. She'd sent the Valkyrie after the sword while I left the key unprotected.

Groaning, I crawled across the floor and then leaned on the windowsill to peer outside.

An angel took flight, the key in his grasp, all three of them dangling precariously.

"You," I muttered, slamming a fist into the glass. My brother, which one, I had no idea. If they were taking the key, that meant they were working for Mom.

The most dangerous goddess in all the realms had the key to the Gates of Hell. I'd fallen for her trap, and now I risked losing it all.

THIRTEEN

"It's...amazing." Levi's voice was laced with admiration and awe.

I grinned at him.

Shaking his head, he was oblivious of the fact that I studied him closely. "More than amazing. Breathtaking even. I had no idea."

"No one ever does." The Gates of Hell weren't what you'd expect. They stood majestically at fifty feet tall and had an outer black marble circle with a rotating inner band of red marble. In the very center, a void of shimmering blue, continually moving, changing, neither water nor air, but a substance born of the universe. That blue was the beginning of creation itself.

Levi raised a hand, fingers reaching out. I knew

the pull the Gates had. They mesmerized you, lured you in with their unique beauty and the sense that something beautiful would be revealed if you just touched it.

I snagged his wrist and held firm. "I wouldn't. Touching the Gate is a direct invitation to the pit."

His eyebrows slammed together. "Seriously?"

"Deadly." Anyone who tried to mess with the Gates of Hell got a one-way ticket to Hell.

"What do the symbols mean?" He pointed to the sigils engraved in the slowly rotating circle. Nine different shapes, each keeping its own secret.

"Part of the combination." The Gates energy thrummed as the blue material arched through the air toward me, wanting my attention and touch. "I know," I soothed, stepping closer, reaching in, and letting the substance encase my hand and arm.

"You're immune?"

"Yes. See the blue? It's the first molecule Hell was built upon. It's also in the mark of the key, connecting us all. It makes me immune." To destroy the gate was to destroy Hell itself. And I'd never let that happen. No matter what my mother threw at me, I wouldn't let her have this.

"It's so different to Heaven's." Levi stood

mesmerized, and his words backed me from the edge of my anger and back to him.

"Yes. The Pearly Gates is more symbolic than anything else." Sucking in a calming breath, I closed my eyes to communicate with the Gate. Strengthening our bond, I delivered a warning.

They're coming.

"Does she know? Does Lilith know how stunning the Gate is? The power? For it has to be powerful, right?" He held up a trembling arm. "I can feel it...look. The hairs on my arm are standing on end."

"Yes. It's very powerful," I agreed, running my hand over his skin and soothing down the hairs that were indeed standing upright. "And no, she doesn't know."

"What?" His eyebrows shot into his hairline. "How did you keep that from her?"

I shrugged. "It never came up. The Gates are sacred. They are the heart of Hell, the essence."

"And the key? Obviously, the key isn't a conventional key, and the Gates aren't conventional gates. What happens when the key and the gate come together?"

"You don't want to know."

"You've trusted me with this, Lucy. Trust me a bit more and tell the truth. What happens?"

I opened my mouth to answer and then clamped it shut. I could feel Ashliel's energy searching for me. She'd never been here, I'd kept the Gate's exact location hidden from her, and I wasn't about to change that.

"We need to go. Ashliel is looking for me." I grabbed Levi's hand and pulled him with me. "Guards!"

Three red dragons appeared, circling overhead. "Your majesty?" they said in unison.

Levi's jaw dropped, and I shrugged. I'd been called worse.

"The Gate is under threat," I said. "The key has been taken. You need to be extra vigilant."

The three of them breathed fire as if outraged that I'd even suggest they hadn't. "We are always vigilant."

"I know you are. But I'm telling you, you need to be *extra* vigilant. An attack is coming. Be prepared. Don't let the Gates fall."

"Ona byr gondtoby xardayk, ona soy uira."

"What was that?" Levi hissed as we walked away.

I glanced at him. "What?"

"What they said. That was a different language, wasn't it?"

"It's the ancient language of my father's childhood."

"Of the gods?"

"Yes. It roughly translates as: *we swear on our lives, we will not fail.*"

"Geez, you really are old." The words tumbled out unheeded, and I bit my lip from laughing at the look of horror on his face when he realized what he'd said. "I mean, I didn't mean..." he stammered, obviously flustered.

"It's okay, I knew what you meant, and yes, I really am old." I swept a hand down the line of my tight form. "Not bad for my age, eh?" I winked at him, tugged him against me, and then flew us away from the Gate and back to Hell HQ.

"There you are!" Ashliel hurried towards us as we stepped into my office. I shot Levi a warning look, reminding him not to reveal where we had been. Turning my attention to Ashliel, I asked, "Any update?"

"Another door has been opened."

I sighed. "Of course. Do we know what and where?"

"Not sure what yet. But I know where. Peru." She glanced at Levi. "Are you going with her?"

Her simple question triggered a light bulb moment. Lilith wanted me to go after the witnesses she was calling. She wanted me out of Hell. "No!" I shouted, making them both jump. They turned surprised faces to me as I paced back and forth. "This is what she wants. She wants me chasing after the witness. She wants me distracted and out of the way. She wants Hell vulnerable."

Ashliel sniffed and jutted her chin in the air. "Well, *I'm* still here."

My head tilted as I considered the frown pulling her brows together and the tight grip she had on her clipboard.

"Yes, you are, and you're a great help. I'd be lost without you. But this is personal. She's coming after Hell, and she's coming after me."

"But you're her daughter," Levi pointed out.

"Yes. I am. But I'm also my father's daughter, and maybe she's decided that since I haven't sided with her, I'm against her. Who knows, really? I need to talk to her, have a conversation and sort this ridiculous mess out."

"Oh," Ashliel whispered.

My gaze narrowed on her. "What?"

"She did send through some requests to meet with you and I…"

I sucked in a breath and kept my temper tucked beneath it. "You what?"

"Told her no." She looked agitated, and Ashliel never got agitated. "I thought it was what you wanted, she's been messing with your head, and you and Levi were still sorting things out and didn't need her interference."

"It's okay, Ash. You were looking out for me; I get it. But reach out and request a meeting, okay? On Earth. Not here, she cannot come here."

"And the witness?" she asked.

"Send the details to Dacian. He can handle this one."

FOURTEEN

"What is this?" Standing before me were Gabriel and Michael. I'd received a message from my mother and returned to Earth to meet with her. Only, upon arrival, I didn't find her. I found them.

Michael unfurled his wings, and I snorted. So, she had returned their powers, as suspected. Gabriel didn't show his wings, but he didn't need to. Instead, he stood back, arms crossed over his chest, a scowl on his face.

"Good to see you, Lucifer," Michael said, his voice carrying an edge to it that said he was anything but glad to see me. Michael inched forward with a smirk on his face and then began circling me, scanning his gaze up and down.

"Where are Del, Jase, and Duke?" I demanded, holding my ground.

He stopped pacing. "Safe. For now."

"So, it *was* you who took them." The feeling of disappointment was unexpected. I'd secretly hoped they weren't involved, but it seemed they were neck-deep in Mother's scheming after all.

"Why are you doing this? Why are you helping her?" I asked, keeping my gaze trained on him.

"The question is, why aren't you?" His lips curled back against his teeth, and I saw the evil in him, a shadow against his soul.

"Because I don't want to destroy Dad and everything he's created, including Hell."

Michael barked out a laugh. "Typical Daddy's girl. Still his favorite, even after what he did, killing your child, you still defend him, stand by him."

It hurt to hear him speak of my baby, but I refused to rise to the bait. I knew the game he was playing; he'd played it before.

"The reason Dad siphoned my magic was that Mom locked him in a hidden cavern for thousands of years. Left him there to rot. Doesn't that mean anything to you? That even then, she was plotting to destroy him."

Michael raised a hand as if to strike me, and I

braced myself, refusing to flinch. Not that I'd let him hit me. I'd have him on the ground in two seconds flat. He must have remembered our last skirmish, for he lowered his hand, clenching it into a fist at his side.

"Just give us what we want, and you can go. You don't need to be involved in this." Michael said.

"Give you the Sword of Souls?" I scoffed, truly amused that they'd think I'd hand it over. "No."

"What if I gave you my word we would keep you out of this?" He shot back.

With one brow raised, I eyed him, wondering if he thought I'd fall for his lies again. With a snort, I said, "You think I am a fool? That I don't know you intend for Hell to fall, along with Earth? Hell is my realm, my home. Don't think I won't defend it with everything I have."

Michael's gaze met mine, and a shiver danced over my skin. There was something dark in the depth of his eyes, something that went deep. Wincing at the pain of how lost he was, I glanced over his shoulder at Gabriel. Was he lost, too? He hadn't said a word, just stood there and let Michael do the talking, the threatening.

"Gabriel?" I asked, wanting his opinion, wanting to know if he stood against me, too.

Michael looked at Gabriel and gave a slight shake of his head.

So, Gabriel was under Michael's command. Well played, he'd had me fooled, all this time letting me think he was trying to help me that Gabriel was the bad apple, manipulating him.

Through narrowed eyes, I studied him, saw the slight flush of color in his cheeks, the clenching of his hands into fists before he relaxed them and pressed them against his thighs.

"You can come with me, Gabriel." I offered. "This doesn't have to be the way."

Michael's backhand across my face surprised me; I hadn't seen it coming. The crack of sound was loud, and the sting in my cheek infuriated me. My wings unfurled, burning with flame, but I didn't retrieve my sword. If I were to fight with Michael, I would do it without the weapon he coveted so badly. He stood, a sneer on his face, and I slapped him.

Hard.

His head snapped back, and one hand rose to his face in surprise.

I smirked. "Stings, doesn't it?"

"Bitch!" he spat.

"Asshole." I kept my voice calm as the temper he

had little control over exploded. There was more to battle than physical combat, yet it seemed Michael had forgotten that as he charged me. We went down in a tangle of limbs, fists flying, sliding along the ground, kicking up gravel as we went. Our blows echoed like thunder overhead, each connection a loud crack, replicating a lightning strike. I was bleeding and breathless, but so was he.

Jumping to my feet, I whirled to face him, only to discover I was no longer on Earth. Instead, I stood in the boardroom of Heaven HQ. Dad stood by the chair at the head of the table, arms crossed over his chest.

"Really, Lucifer, disagreeing with your brothers? Again?"

"Are you serious?" I furled my wings and cleaned myself up, tugging my shirt into place before planting my fists on my hips and eyeballing my father. "You pulled me to Heaven to reprimand me for fighting?"

He sighed and shook his head. "No." Pulling out a chair, he took a seat and then indicated that I do the same.

I took the seat to his left, leaning out of arms reach. I didn't want him to touch me. It was too soon. I was still raw.

"I'm sorry." He looked at me with sad, puppy dog eyes, and my own eyes welled in response. What could I say? That it was okay? I knew he was referring to the transference of my child, my unborn baby. I blinked my tears away, changing the subject.

"You need to do something about Mom," I finally said.

"I know." His voice was pure misery.

I glanced at him with razors in my gaze. This was not the father I remembered. He had been strong. Confident. A ruler.

"I've made such a mess of things, Lucy." He sighed, bowing his head. I looked at him in shock. Disappointment flooded me, followed by anger. He was the creator, he'd made us all, and he was admitting defeat? Without even putting up a fight?

"You need to be the man she fell in love with," I said, tamping down the emotion in my voice. "Strong. Excited to share your life with her, excited for the future, excited for life."

"But I'm not with her anymore. And she sure as Hell doesn't want to be with me."

"Oh no? You think she's going to all this trouble because she doesn't care? She's going to all this trouble because she cares *too* much. You hurt her, Dad. She wants to hurt you in return.

You can't sit back and let her do that because she's not only hurting you, she's killing people. Destroying worlds. You know she's calling the witnesses? Which reminds me, what does that even mean?"

"Calling the witnesses?" He sighed, his fingers twisting the ring on his finger around. "A god—or goddess—can call a meeting of the witnesses to request action be taken against another god. Or goddess. A witness is simply a god—or goddess—not directly involved in whatever conflict has occurred."

"Witnesses are gods?"

"Yes."

"And calling the witnesses is...calling out another god?"

"Sort of. If there is a disagreement that cannot be resolved between gods, if there is a complaint or wrongdoing, then the witnesses are called to make a ruling. A minimum of six witnesses must gather and hear the testimony from the god who feels he—or she—has been wronged."

"Like a court hearing?"

"Exactly. Only the witnesses must agree unanimously that the accused is either guilty or innocent. If guilty, they then decide a punishment, or they have the power to give that power to the accuser."

"So, basically, Mom is taking you to court? To have you officially punished?"

"It appears that way." He looked sadder than I'd ever seen him, his lips turned down at the corners and his eyes flat.

"But...what is she charging you with?"

He shrugged. "I don't know. I guess I will find out if she manages to call together enough witnesses."

"But why is she calling them to Earth? Why not her realm?"

"To hurt me is my best guess."

"Dad," I whispered, horrified. "That is wrong on so many levels."

"Your mother has always been very conniving," Dad admitted, rubbing his chin.

"Michael and Gabriel have the key to the gates of Hell," I said.

"What?" His head snapped up, and he was fully alert. *Finally.*

I nodded. "It's true. I hid the key in three vessels. They've taken them."

"We can't let Hell fall. The gate holds..."

"The essence of the Universe. I know. I won't let

it fall, but I need to be there, protecting it. I can't be running around Earth hunting witnesses and trying to stop Mom. Or my brothers. You need to intervene, Dad. I know you don't want to, I know you think Mom has a right to be angry, but she doesn't have the right to do this. She needs to be stopped, and it's unfair that you expect me to be the one to stop her. She's my mom."

I bit my lip. I'd never spoken to my father in such a direct manner before, but we were approaching crisis point, and he needed to get his head out of his ass and into the game. Lilith was playing to win— she would see our realms annihilated unless we stopped her.

"Returning Heaven to health took a lot out of me." He practically pouted, and I frowned so hard my eyeballs hurt.

Was my father truly a whiny little bitch?

"Suck it up," I scolded. "You said yourself this is all your fault. She's doing this because you pissed her off. Fix it. It's your mess. You clean it up, and stop relying on everyone else to do your dirty work."

His mouth dropped open, and his voice boomed, "Lucifer!"

"No!" I shouted back. "You don't take that tone with me! You are my father; you are God, creator of

Heaven, Hell, and Earth. You don't get to sit here on a gilded throne and not be responsible for your actions. You need to step up. Are you not hearing all the prayers? Even I can hear them, and I'm in Hell! The people are desperate. They need you. Don't fail them. Not again."

His following words surprised me.

"You are so like your mother." There was pride in his voice, and his lips curled in a smile.

I blinked. "And that's a good thing?"

He nodded. "Yes. It's a good thing. She was a good woman, a loving woman, and I neglected her. I made her into what she is today, and you're right. This is my mess. I'll fix it. I'll deal with her."

"And the witnesses?"

Another nod. "And the witnesses. You return to Hell. Guard the gate, for if it falls, we all fall."

"Do you think she knows that? Why else take the key?" My voice was somber, laced with the pain of knowing that my own mother would do something that would hurt me.

"She could quite possibly know," Dad admitted. "I never hid anything from her. She could have seen the blueprints. But we have time. I'll find her. Talk to her. Make her see reason."

I was skeptical. I doubted anything my father

said would appease my mother, but there was one thing we did agree on. He had to sort this out with her.

"And Michael and Gabriel?" I asked. "You do know she gave them back their powers?"

"I'll deal with them after I've dealt with Lilith."

"And what is it you think you'll say? To Mom, that is, because I don't think sorry is going to cut it."

"I'm going to tell her that I love her."

"Do you?"

"I always have. My vows meant something to me. They still do. She's my wife. I didn't mean to hurt her. I didn't realize I was neglecting her, even when she told me, I didn't realize, didn't take her pain seriously."

"Until she left."

"Until she left. And then it was too late. I couldn't get to her. I couldn't speak to her. I couldn't show her I loved her. Still. Always."

"Yet you find it in your heart to forgive her, to love her, despite her locking you in a tomb in Hell for thousands of years?"

"You know the power of love and forgiveness, Lucy." His voice was as soft as a whisper, yet it resonated around us as if he'd shouted the words. "Love trumps everything."

FIFTEEN

Upon returning to Hell, I sought Levi out. Dad's words touched me. Love and forgiveness. For although Levi and I were back together, I felt there was much left unspoken.

"You're back." He smiled in greeting, cupped a hand around my nape, and kissed me. That's when it truly dawned on me, the power this man had over me. Emotion flooded my body, making me warm all over. I kissed him back and then slowly eased away.

"I love you, Levi Forrester," I whispered, resting my forehead against his. "You are my everything, and I will fight for you."

"Hey." He eased away and cupped my face in his hands. "What brought this on?" He grinned. "Not that I'm complaining."

"I was talking with Dad about him and my mom. And get this, he still loves her. He's always loved her. Yet, he let her leave him. He didn't fight. Not hard enough, anyway. And now look at the result."

Levi was silent a moment, digesting what I'd said. "I love you, too. With all my heart. Both human and demon. I know I hurt you, and for that, I'm truly sorry. You'll never appreciate how deeply sorry I am." His eyes glistened, and my breath caught in my throat.

"You didn't mean to. I forgive you," I whispered, kissing him again, my own tears sliding down my cheeks.

"You are my world. Without you, I'm nothing." His words breathed against my lips and made my knees buckle. I felt it then, our bond, growing tighter. He gasped, and I looked at him.

"What is it?"

"My mark." He tugged at his shirt, trying to see his shoulder. "It burned."

"Let me see." I turned him around and pulled his shirt up to reveal my mark on his shoulder.

"Wow," I mumbled, tracing my fingers over the symbol.

"What is it?" He peered at me over his shoulder.

"You know how it was black?"

"Mmhm."

"It's now gold." I placed a kiss on the mark and smoothed his shirt back down.

Turning back around, he asked, "It changes colors?"

"Apparently."

"The closer we get, the more it grows." He nodded as if it all made perfect sense.

"I'm still not sure about the whole kid issue," I admitted, knotting my hands together.

He wrapped my hands in his, stilling my agitated movements. "Babe, we have all the time in the world. We're both immortal. There's no rush. Whenever you're ready, we'll try for another baby."

"We didn't try for this one," I pointed out.

He grinned, giving me a wink. "Exactly."

"Wait!" I peered at him with narrowed eyes. "What do you mean by that?"

"It will happen when it is meant to happen. Stop stressing. You'll make an awesome mom. When the time is right."

"It's scary how you have utter faith in me," I grumbled, taking him by the hand and leading him toward the bedroom. We were almost at the door when the building shook. I gasped, bending my knees to keep my balance as everything around us vibrated.

"Earthquake?" Levi guessed, his eyes round.

"No. Someone is attacking the Gate. I've got to go." Before he could reply, I spread my wings. I materialized moments later at the Gates of Hell, only to discover my dragons in battle with my brothers.

One dragon remained steadfast in front of the Gate while the remaining two grappled with my brothers overhead. I flew in to stand next to the grounded dragon, sword drawn should he be defeated.

"Michael. Gabriel," I shouted over the clang of swords and the harsh rush of beating wings. "Enough!"

They both glanced my way and then at each other. Moments passed in silent communication before they nodded and then descended to stand in front of me. My dragons remained in the air, on guard and breathing fire. They were not happy that two angels had made it this far, had made it to the Gate, and the fury in their eyes told me they were seconds from turning Michael and Gabriel into crispy critters.

"You don't want to do this," I told them, not

missing how their gazes lingered on the Sword of Souls still grasped in my hand. I didn't want to use it on them, but I would if they backed me into a corner.

They backed me into a corner.

With what I can only describe as a warrior yell, they launched at me. I swung my blade, clashing it against Michael's while overhead, the dragons unleashed their fire. Amongst the chaos of screams, searing flesh, clashing swords, and beating wings, we fought. Michael stayed on me, despite his burns, while Gabriel took on the dragons. Distracting them, drawing them away. A smart tactic, one I would have used myself if our positions were reversed.

I had the upper hand. Dragon fire did not hurt me; I was immune to flame. Michael was not, and although he had healed himself, he'd used precious energy to do so. When I ducked low and darted behind him, he swiveled to follow, losing his footing. One simple kick to his knee, and he toppled. I stood over him, the tip of my blade resting against his chest.

"Do it," he puffed, eyes dark with hate. "Kill me. End it."

I hesitated. I couldn't do it, couldn't kill my own

brother, and from the way one corner of his lip curled up, he knew it. Despite everything, he was my family.

"Still as weak as ever, Lucifer," he drawled. "But don't be fooled. When the time comes, I won't hesitate."

"You'd kill me?" His threat surprised me. Sure, we had our fights, our disagreements, and I thought he was a total douche, but I never thought he hated me so much that he'd kill me.

"Wouldn't hesitate," he confirmed. "Unlike you. *Now!*"

His shout startled me just as much as the sweep of his arm that dislodged my sword from his chest did. He unfurled his wings and flew out of reach while I stood in stunned disbelief as a tear appeared in Hell's veil.

Angel after angel flooded into Hell, swords drawn. He'd created an army. Or Lilith had.

"Ashliel!" I yelled, shooting into the air and engaging in battle. "Reinforcements to the Gate."

If she responded, I didn't hear over the noise.

Swooping through the air, I dispatched angel after angel, only to have another three take their place. We were vastly outnumbered, and my heart chilled at the thought that Hell could very well fall.

One of my dragons crashed to the ground, dozens of swords protruding from his body. His gaze tracked me, bleak and full of apology, as his dying breath left his body in a puff of smoke.

"No!" I screamed, racing to his side, but it was too late. They'd killed my dragon. The four of us had been together since day one. I'd never expected to lose one and not under these circumstances. Steeling my spine, I returned to the fray, anger fueling me, when a sudden influx of angels in black armor flew through the rift, led by Dacian. Reinforcements at last.

"Ashliel! Where the Hell are you? Respond!" I barked the order, knowing she could hear me through our connection. Why wasn't she responding? Had something happened? Was Hell HQ under attack also? But if that were the case, she'd have sounded the alarm. Had they captured her? Rendered her helpless, or worse, killed her? And if they had, what of Levi? I had left him in the penthouse, was he also captured?

My imagination went wild, distracting me with worst-case scenarios, so I wasn't prepared when an angel landed on my back, locked his legs around my waist, and drew a sword to my throat. With my wings incapacitated, we tumbled to the ground, falling hard. Although I had the wind knocked out of me, I didn't hesitate, pushing up and dislodging the angel, swinging my sword hard. My weapon connected with his neck, and his head toppled, hitting the ground with a thump and rolling away.

"Lucy! Watch out!" Dacian shouted, and I swiveled, raising my sword in time to deflect a blow aimed at my head. Dacian landed behind me, and we stood back-to-back, slowly circling and dispatching angels one by one. Covered in sweat and panting with exhaustion, we kept going. Their numbers were dwindling; I still had two dragons in play who turned the angels into barbecued snacks. The stench embedded in my nostrils, and the air was thick with smoke. Ignoring the sting in my eyes, I sharpened my focus.

"Urg." The grunt from Dacian, followed by the sound of him crashing to his knees, caught my attention.

Keeping my sword raised, I maneuvered to him, doing my best to keep the angels at bay. But they sensed weakness, they smelled his blood, and knew, just as I did, that his wound was severe.

"I'm hit," he gurgled, looking at me with surprise in his eyes while blood trickled from his mouth.

Shit.

"Can you heal?" I grabbed his arm and tried to pull him to his feet, but he was dead weight.

The angels circled in closer.

"Dacian?" I whispered, fear freezing me. "You can't be dying." I shook him. "Heal yourself!" I cried out, deflecting a blow meant for him. I stood over him, a foot on either side of his hips, as he leaned forward onto my thigh, his blood seeping through my pants and bathing my skin in warm wetness.

"Dacian? Dacian?" I screamed, nudging him with my knee and gasping when his body fell back, his eyes open, staring at nothing, his chest immobile. I froze, my gaze locked on the body of my best friend. Without conscious thought, I dropped to my knees and released my sword to cradle his face in my hands.

"Dacian? Come on, please, heal yourself...heal yourself..." My whisper was choked with tears as I rubbed his cheeks, his eyes blank, not seeing. He'd never see anything again. He was gone, and my heart shattered. I'd lost too much today. My faithful dragon and my best friend. I couldn't allow this to continue, my brothers had crossed the line, and despite my earlier reluctance to kill them, now all I wanted was their blood. I would kill every last one of them.

I was reaching for my sword and didn't see the blow coming. Thundering pain sliced into my temples. Then I began to fall into the deepest darkness.

SIXTEEN

"Come on…wake up."

It took me a moment to place the sweet feminine voice near my ear. My head pounded, and I sent a shot of magic to the source of my pain, felt my scalp repair itself, and then slowly blinked open my eyes. Del leaned over me, concern on her face.

"Are you alright?" Her voice shook ever so slightly, and I gave her a reassuring smile.

"I'm fine. All healed." I sat up, and she moved back, giving me space.

"Where are we?" I asked, glancing around, trying to place the purple room, only to realize I'd never been in it before. It was as if someone had vomited purple, for the walls, floor, even the ceiling, was bathed in it, except for one wall, which was clear glass. Outside the glass window was a corridor, grey with a gold stripe running down the center. On the opposite side of the aisle was a room identical to this one.

Pressing my face against the glass, I peered farther down the corridor. More rooms. Just like this one. Only they weren't rooms...they were cells. But we didn't have cells like this in Hell. Or Heaven. Or Earth.

"We don't know," Del replied, moving to sit next to Jase, who was sitting on a single bed that was pushed up against the wall. Duke was curled up by his side. The key was here—together and alive.

"Are you sure you're okay? That's a lot of blood." Jase pointed at my pants, and I glanced down.

Yep.

A lot of blood.

Dacian's blood.

The memory of his death flooded my brain, and tears welled up. I struggled to comprehend he was gone, that my brothers were responsible for his death, that they'd stoop so low. It all happened so fast, and I hadn't been able to heal him.

"The bloods not mine." Using my magic, I cleaned myself up and changed outfits. "My magic works, so I propose I get us out of here. What do you say?"

The only response was a low, feminine giggle, and the sound knotted my muscles with fear.

"That sounds like a wonderful plan, Lucifer, my dear; only you should know that you can't leave here. Not without my permission. And I do not give it." It was a female voice that spoke from outside our cell.

I gulped. "Mother?"

The woman who had given birth to me strolled regally down the walkway between the cells. She was dressed in a purple and gold gown, complete with a crown on her head and a staff in her hand. She looked like a queen, and my mouth dropped open at the sight of her. It sounded corny, but she was magnificent like she'd stepped straight out of a fairy tale. And clearly, she was a lover of the color purple.

"Welcome home." She stopped outside my cell and smiled at me. I saw myself in that smile. In appearance, we were very similar. But as far as I'm concerned, that was as far as it went. Inside, where it counted, we were a sword and feather. Different, in every way.

"Let me out," I demanded, unflinchingly meeting her gaze.

She chuckled and shook her head. "Sorry, my darling, I can't do that. You'll try and stop me."

"Because you need to be stopped." I stabbed the glass with my finger. "What you're doing is wrong."

She banged the staff down hard on the floor, and the crack shook the walls, making my ears ring. "Silence." Her voice dripped authority and ice, and I swallowed, unnerved. "This is my realm, and you will respect me as your Queen."

It was an order. One I couldn't follow. I didn't voice my thoughts since I was reasonably sure that she was unhinged and antagonizing her wouldn't be the smartest move.

"Thank you for not harming them," I said instead, indicating Del, Jase, and Duke, who sat huddled together on the bed, staring with wide eyes.

"Pft. They are of no importance. I took them to lure you here, but you didn't take the bait. And now, I don't need them at all."

"You don't?"

"Hell has fallen. It is no more. Therefore, I don't need the key." She waved a hand in dismissal while my mouth hung open.

"Hell can't be gone," I whispered, not sure how much more bad news I could take.

"Let me assure you, it most certainly is. Don't believe me? Watch." She waved her hand, and a vision appeared in the air, an image of the battle in Hell. Michael flew in behind me while I was bent over Dacian's body and hit me in the temple with the butt of his sword. Scooping me up around the waist, he flew away. I assumed he had brought me here.

With Dacian and I gone, the Gate was breached within seconds. The vision changed, showing Hell HQ tumble over the edge of the cliff it was perched on, the buildings surrounding it crumbling in response. Streams of souls fled the pit, heading toward the Gate now that it was open. The shimmering blue essence gone. They just had to step through, and they would return to Earth as Revenants.

God help us all.

"Why?" I whispered, tears falling. I prayed that Levi had gotten out, that he'd return to Earth. I still felt our bond, so I knew he wasn't dead, but I worried for him and knew he would be searching for me.

"Because it is his creation, and it must be destroyed. All of it."

"Mom," I pleaded. "Talk to Dad. Please. It doesn't have to be like this. He loves you. He still loves you."

She laughed, a high-pitched hysterical sound, then leveled me with her gaze. I couldn't help but shiver. "I gave up everything for him. My family. My realm. Everything. And he abandoned me for his puny creations. His animals. His worlds. Everything was more important to him than me."

"He made mistakes, sure, but he's sorry. Mom, please. Just talk to him."

"He will pay."

"He's already paid. You locked him in a tomb, for Heaven's sake. Left him to rot."

"That was just the beginning," she hissed, cracking the staff on the floor once more. "There is so much more to come. I will take everything he holds dear, every human, every creature, every living thing, every atom from his precious collection will be destroyed."

"And me? What about me, Mom? I'm a part of him."

"You are my daughter. I'll not harm you." She nodded as if confirming her words.

"But you are hurting me!" I cried. "This…" I waved my arm around the cell. "This hurts me. Locking me up hurts me. Destroying Hell hurts me. Hell was my realm. You took my home." My heart hurt at the knowledge that Hell was gone. She'd destroyed it. I was sure anger would fill me soon enough, but at that moment, all I felt was deep intense sadness.

"*This* is your home. And it's high time you came home, to where you belong."

"I don't belong here, Mom. No more than Michael and Gabriel do. I assume they're here?"

"They are good boys." She smiled, nodding.

"They are evil assholes, is what they are," I ground out, frustration making me want to punch the glass separating us.

"Enough." Her voice dripped ice, and she struck the floor with her staff again. I cringed at the sound. "Until you can be civil, you will stay here." She turned away before stopping to address one of her guards. "Dispose of the key."

"What? No! Mom, wait!" I banged frantically against the glass.

She stopped and looked at me over her shoulder, one brow perfectly arched. "What is it?"

Barely able to catch my breath, I said, "Spare them. Please. For me."

She looked at me for several seconds and then turned and walked away without a word.

I blinked. What did that mean? That Del, Jase, and Duke were spared? For now, at least? Or not? I closed my eyes on a sigh, resting my forehead against the glass. What a mess.

Gathering my strength, I turned. Still huddled on the bed, they stared at me, unmoving. "Come on, we don't have much time. I need to get you out of here." My voice was harsher than I intended, but it made them move. Scooting off the bed, they stood together, Jase with his arm around Del, keeping her pinned to his side, Duke's collar firmly clasped in his other hand.

I stepped up to them and wrapped my wings around them. The magical restrictions of the cell pressed down on me, and I knew I wouldn't be able to fly out. Still, I'd used my magic to heal myself and change my clothes, so hopefully, flight was the only power I couldn't use. I prayed I had enough in reserve to teleport them out of the purple room.

Holding my breath, I closed my eyes and concentrated. Hard. The air stirred, and my hair blew back from my face. There was a gasp, and when I opened my eyes, they were gone. I'd sent them to Heaven. But, using my magic to save them drained me, and I staggered, light-headed and dizzy. Making my way to the bed, I laid down, snuggling into the warmth Jase, Del, and Duke had left behind. I'd saved them, but I hadn't been able to save myself. I'd tried to go with them, but something held me here. I was shackled to this realm.

A day passed. Then another. No one came. Either they didn't know the key was gone, or they didn't care. Finally, I admitted to myself that if Hell had indeed fallen, then my mother wouldn't need the key at all. She planned to kill them and probably still would, but they had a chance at survival, at least in Heaven.

As the hours slowly ticked by, the sadness and shock that Hell had fallen wore off, and anger took its place. I stared at the ridiculous purple ceiling, seething with frustration and pain. How dare she? Couldn't she see that what she had done, destroying Hell, hurt me? Didn't she know it cut me to the bone? She was my mother. *No more*, I swore to myself; I'd no longer view her as my mother. She was Lilith. A deranged semi-God from another dimension that was a threat and had to be destroyed.

Another day passed, and my anger subsided to a slow burn. My thoughts turned to Levi, bringing me a sense of comfort. I could feel him through our bond. He was alive, wherever he was, and I vowed I would get out of this place and return to him. We'd rebuild Hell. Together with Ashliel, the three of us would make it stronger than ever.

I steadfastly kept my thoughts away from Dacian, for each time his face appeared in my mind, I'd cry, and the tears were starting to burn my cheeks. Anger at Lilith warred with the grief over the loss of my best friend and my home.

I'd given up trying to track time when my brothers arrived outside my cell. I looked them up and down, screwed up my nose at their silver pants and purple shirts. I couldn't help it; I burst out laughing.

"Have you two seen yourselves?" I finally got myself under control, wiping tears of laughter from my eyes. "You look ridiculous! I mean, what is that? A seventies throwback? And why are you dressed like twins?"

"It's the Royal robes," Gabriel muttered, a blush staining his cheeks.

"Where are the robes, then? I mean, the knee-high silver boots that practically blend with your pants are a nice touch, but maybe a robe would…" I laughed again, unable to finish my sentence, bending at the waist and holding my side.

"Shut up!" Michael snapped. "It pleases Mother that we wear the colors of Toqith, her realm."

"I thought she was from Qanyl?" I remembered childhood stories about her home.

Michael shook his head. "Qanyl is her family's realm. She created her own dimension, Toqith, when she left Heaven."

I suppose I should have been grateful for the explanation, glad that he was speaking to me at all, but the truth was, I was the one locked in a cell, and he and Gabriel were standing outside of it. Granted, they were dressed like clowns, and I had to bite the inside of my cheek to keep from laughing again, but if I wanted freedom, I needed allies. They were my best bet. The power of three.

"So, you here to finally let me out or what?" I cocked a brow, curious to their intent. Gabriel wouldn't look at me, while Michael was happy to meet my gaze and scowl.

"Mother isn't happy," Michael said.

"Oh?"

"You rescued the key."

"Ah, so she did notice that?"

"You shouldn't have been able to do that. It made her angry that you did."

"So?" I shrugged. Like I was going to let her hurt my friends. Like I'd sit back and do nothing.

"You have to be punished." There was that note of glee in Michael's voice again, one that told me he was really enjoying this—and that it was very possible I wouldn't like what he had to say next.

"Punished how? I'm already locked in a cell."

A grin split his face. "It's time for the Dungeon."

It turns out he was right. I didn't like what he said. I looked from him to Gabriel—who still wouldn't look at me—and back again.

"Are you insane? A dungeon? As in...torture?" I knew as soon as the words left my mouth that I was right. They intended to torture me. To inflict pain. Only, Gabriel didn't look so thrilled about it. Zeroing in on him, I pleaded, "Gabriel, come on. Surely, you're not on board with this? You're going to torture me?"

"It is law," he muttered, tugging at the collar of his shirt, unable to cast his gaze in my direction.

"Gabriel! Don't let them do this to me. I'm your sister!" I wasn't above begging because I had a feeling the torture Michael had in mind would be beyond horrifying. Whatever spell Lilith put on the cell was amped up, for I couldn't use my magic at all anymore. I assumed she'd done that when she discovered I'd spirited Del, Jase, and Duke away. Which meant any pain inflicted would not instantly heal. Injuries wouldn't magically disappear. This was going to suck. I knew it, Gabriel knew it, and Michael most certainly knew it.

The glass wall between us disappeared, and I was pulled out by two guards, who wrenched my arms so tight behind my back that I feared they might pop clean out of their sockets.

"Easy." I winced. "I'm going to need those later."

"Later?" Michael raised a brow, enjoying my discomfort.

"Yeah. When I punch you in the face."

Restrained as I was, I had nowhere to go when he punched me. In the face. *Oh, the irony.* Pain ricocheted across my cheekbones, and my nose smashed inward. Definitely broken. A second later, blood was flowing over my lips and down my chin.

"Ouch," I muttered. "Make you feel good hitting a girl? A restrained girl? What a hero."

"Michael." The warning in Gabriel's voice was unmistakable. He wasn't on board with this. If there was a weakness to be had, it was Gabriel. He'd always been the follower, Michael the leader, and maybe, just maybe, this wasn't what Gabriel wanted. He could be my ticket out of here. I just needed to get him alone to get him onside.

"If you don't have the stomach for this, then leave," Michael snapped, wrapping his fingers around my upper arm and dragging me forward, knowing full well his grip hurt.

I didn't give him the satisfaction of wincing, although I couldn't help a deflated feeling when Gabriel walked away in the opposite direction. So much for getting him alone.

SEVENTEEN

The dungeon really was a dungeon. It was dark, dank, and suitably horrifying. I filed a mental note to build my own dungeon in Hell for the sinners. Just being in this place was unnerving. Gone were the purple, golds, and silvers of Lilith's preferred décor. The dungeon was stone and rock, windowless. The only light came from the occasional wall sconce that cast eerie shadows across the walls.

And it was big. Who knew Lilith needed such facilities. Maybe her followers weren't as loyal as she would like, for the blood on the floor was fresh, the coppery tang of it still hung in the air.

The room itself was round, with half a dozen rooms around the perimeter, metal bars exposing the cells to the torture chamber in the center. There was no sugar coating what went on here, for in the very center of the dungeon were two wooden beams, crossing in the middle to form an X, chains dangling. This was where you were tortured. I didn't need to be told; I could see the stains in the wood.

"Chain her," Michael ordered.

I wasn't going to stand by and accept my fate.

No way.

I was Lucifer, Queen of Hell, and no one was going to chain me up and torture me.

I spun in the guard's grip, facing him, my arm slipping from his grasp when I took him by surprise. I headbutted him, the crack echoing off the stone walls. He staggered backward from the impact. I ignored the pain in my forehead and turned on the other guard, who charged, flipping him over my shoulder. They were novices. Easily dispatched. I'd be out of here in seconds. I was sure of it. That was until Michael pressed something into my lower back, and what can only be described as a bolt of lightning shot through my body.

I went rigid, unable to move, toppling to the ground. I twitched and groaned, the pain unimaginable. Through watering eyes, I eyeballed the staff that I hadn't noticed Michael carrying earlier. It was similar to Lilith's but smaller and clearly a weapon.

"Get up!" Michael snapped at the guards who jumped to obey. I was dragged up and chained to the wooden boards, my toes barely touching the ground. The pain of the electric shock was fading, giving me the chance to focus on my anger.

"Low blow Michael," I ground out.

"We're only just beginning," he promised, and I swallowed, a tiny edge of panic seeping in. With my magic suppressed, so were my healing abilities. He could kill me here, and I had a sinking feeling that was his intention. He'd make it look like an accident, make it look like he hadn't intended for things to go quite that far. I could see it in his eyes. His hatred for me and his love of inflicting pain radiated out of him in waves.

He was the type to kill kittens. He was like the boys on the beach who were going to burn Nibbler alive. Evil. Closing my eyes, I prayed. I prayed that I'd survive this, I prayed that Levi was safe, I prayed Mr. Meow and Nibbler were okay, I prayed for Heaven, Hell, and Earth. And I prayed God would hear me and come to the rescue because I was screwed.

"Are you...praying?" Michael laughed in disbelief.

"I am." No point in denying it. Prayer was a powerful thing; it would be foolish of him to discount it.

"Oh, you stupid girl. No one is listening. No one cares. Least of all, Dad."

I didn't reply as he walked over to a bench, laid his staff upon it, and then ran his hands over a selection of knives. Big knives. Sharp-looking knives. Next to the blades were other things. Things with pointy ends and hooks and barbs. I blinked, not wanting to think about what they could do to a body.

Finally selecting a knife, he picked it up and tossed it over and over in his hand, each time catching it expertly by the handle despite my intent wish that he'd misstep and slice his palm. Then he was in front of me, and I swallowed.

"Ready?" he drawled, resting the cold blade against my cheek.

"Bring it." I kept my teeth clenched and vowed I wouldn't scream. He wanted me to scream; I couldn't give him the satisfaction. He drew it out; rather than cutting my flesh with the knife, he ripped my shirt from my body, then my pants, leaving me decidedly vulnerable in my underwear.

I shivered, realizing he'd done this before. Many times. He'd honed his skills at torture, and I wondered where my brother, the young boy who had been fun and carefree, had gone.

He reached up and slowly dragged the tip of the blade down the inside of my arm, from wrist to armpit.

I screwed my eyes shut, clamped my lips closed, and breathed in deep through my nose. It hurt like a bitch, but I didn't scream. I could feel the wetness of my blood run down my side, its scent reaching my nostrils, making me want to gag, but I held steadfast. I would not scream.

Michael chuckled, "I knew you wouldn't. I knew you would be my biggest challenge." He traced the blade over my face, not cutting, just freaking me the fuck out. My eyes sprang open. I needed something to focus on. Not him. Not me. Not the pain. I zeroed in on the wall and gave it my utmost attention while he cut my other arm from wrist to armpit. No screaming. *Good Lucifer. You're doing good.*

He kept true to his word. He was good at this, and he was having a ball. I wish I could say the same, but alas, I felt much like a shredded ribbon and feared I looked the same.

"Enough!" I thought it was Gabriel's outraged voice I heard, but I couldn't be sure. All I knew was the cutting stopped. But the bleeding didn't. I was cut open, dying. He didn't need to pierce an organ to kill me. Draining my body of all its blood would do it.

My ears were blocked, everything muffled. I was fading fast. Just as I was drawing my last breath, blessed relief lifted me from the darkness. My flesh began knitting back together, a familiar tingling danced across my skin. I was being healed.

Fuck. He was healing me to start again. I hadn't thought of that, and I almost cried at the injustice of it all.

Only it *was* Gabriel's voice I heard. "I'm so sorry, Lucy."

With a monumental effort, I dragged my eyelids open and peered into the face of my other brother. I had no words as I stared into his sorrowful eyes. He held my gaze as he continued to heal me, then my wrists were released from the chains, and I fell into his arms. Healed, I may be, but I was still suffering from blood loss. I couldn't stand on my own.

"Mother said she was to be punished." Michael

sounded all pouty as he stood by his bench of torture devices.

"Not like this. Not to death," Gabriel spat, striding out of the dungeon with me in his arms. I tried to keep my eyes open, unlock my aching jaw to speak to him, but it was too much. I had zero strength. Instead, my head flopped back, and I passed out.

When I came to, I wasn't in my cell like I'd been expecting. Instead, I was on a massive bed in an over-the-top opulent room. Raising a hand, I felt across my abdomen, checked my ribs were still in place, noticed I was dressed in some sort of silk fabric, and knew without looking it would be purple. I couldn't hide my surprise when I finally opened my eyes to look and discovered I was dressed in a gown of white.

"You're awake."

"Thank you, Captain Obvious." I turned my head on the pillow to look at Gabriel, who was sitting in a chair pulled up to the side of the bed.

"Feeling better?" he asked, ignoring my sarcasm.

"Yes. But if you're waiting for me to thank you for saving me, don't hold your breath." I sat up and scooted to the far side of the bed, away from him.

He chuckled, but there was no humor in the sound. "And if you're waiting for an apology, ditto."

I stood up and faced him, idly smoothing the white gown over my hips. It was really rather lovely but not something I'd wear unless I was going to a ball. And I had absolutely no intentions of going to a ball anytime soon.

"You let him take me," I pointed out. "You could have stopped him then and there, but you let him take me. I think that deserves an apology."

He was silent for a moment, watching me. He hadn't moved from his chair, which was a good thing because despite him healing me and taking me from the dungeon, I wasn't sure I could trust him. This could all be a trick. Punishment of a different sort. One to play with my mind, with my emotions.

"You broke the rules. You had to be punished."

"Considering I don't know the rules, that's a trifle unfair, wouldn't you say?"

He cocked his head then nodded. "Fair enough. But I'm sure you had a fair idea that spiriting them out of here wasn't going to be acceptable to mother."

This time I nodded. "True. So...what now? Is this my new cell? Did I get an upgrade?" I waved an arm around the room, full of French-inspired furniture, tapestries, lush carpet, and thick velvet drapes. Purple, of course.

"This is a guest room. If you misbehave, you'll be returned to your cell."

"And if I behave?"

"Then you have free reign of the castle. Within reason."

"The castle? We're in a castle?" I rushed to the window, pushed the drapes aside to look outside. What I saw sucked the breath from my lungs. We were perched on top of a mountain. I could see part of the castle—it was huge, and below us, down in the valley, I could see a silver city. In the skies flew dragons of every imaginable size and color.

"Wow." I breathed. It was breathtakingly beautiful. "So, this is Toqith?"

"Yes. Your new home."

He'd come to stand by my side, to look out over our mother's kingdom. I shook my head. "This is not my home," I said. "It will never be my home. She may force me to stay, strip me of my powers, but I will be waiting, watching for a way to leave, for this is nothing more than a gilded prison to me. I have my own home to get back to."

"Hell is gone," he said flatly.

"I don't believe that." I couldn't. For if I gave up the notion that Hell couldn't be saved, then I'd fall into a pit of despair so bottomless I'd never climb out. I had to believe I could rebuild. For Levi was there. I could still feel our bond and knew he was there. Surviving. Waiting for me. And I would move Heaven and Earth to return to him; I'd never rest in my quest to be with the man I love.

"Then you are foolish."

"Gabriel, what has become of you?" I turned to him then, clasped his hands in mine, truly anguished at what had become of my brother. "Michael is lost, I can see that his soul is tainted, and there is no saving him, but you? You are good. How can you let this happen? How can you help them? Lilith is destroying all that we hold dear."

"She is our mother. We owe her our loyalty." He wouldn't meet my eyes, instead looking over my head at the vista outside.

"And what of Father? Do we not owe him loyalty?"

"I..."

The door opened before he could finish, and Ashliel strode in, red hair blazing.

"Ashliel!" I'd never been happier to see her. "You found me! Tell me it isn't true. Hell isn't fallen!" Not giving her time to answer, I spun to Gabriel. "See! Hell can't be fallen if Ashliel is here to rescue me." Back to Ashliel. "Is Lilith captured?"

Gabriel barked out a laugh, and I looked at him in surprise.

"Oh, Lucy." He was shaking his head, his eyes back to being puppy dog sad.

"What?" I looked from him to Ashliel and back again. "What's going on?"

Ignoring me, Ashliel crossed to Gabriel and slapped him on the back. "Good to see you again, Gabe."

Gabe? She called him Gabe? Were they...friends?

"Look at her face...it's priceless." She chuckled, laughing at me. Laughing. *At me*. I frowned. What the fuck was going on here?

"Just tell her," Gabriel muttered, looking uncomfortable.

"Oh, fine. You spoil all my fun." Flicking her hair over her shoulder, she faced me head-on and said, "The truth is, Lucifer, I'm with Lilith. Always have been from day one. You were right thinking you had a spy in Hell. *Tadaa!* That spy is me, fooled you— fooled you all."

My mouth dropped open. I had no words. None. I was numb with the shock of her betrayal. All along, she'd been spying on me for Lilith? My friend, my second in command, was a traitor? I was shaking my head, unable to believe it.

"But...you...when? How?"

"Lilith and I were friends in Heaven before she left. She knew things were going south with your dad, so when he put you in charge of Hell, she asked me to go with you, keep an eye on things, help her put her plan into motion." Ashliel shrugged as if it were no big deal.

I sat on the edge of the bed, unable to believe what I was hearing.

"Oh, look, she's gone comatose." I'd never heard Ashliel's voice so gleeful. How had I missed this? I looked at her now with narrowed eyes. She let the façade drop, and I could see the evil surrounding her, like poison, like Michael. Her eyes were dark with it. Her hair no longer flamed; instead, it flowed over her shoulder in sleek tresses of chocolate brown with just a hint of purple. Lilith's color. She bore Lilith's color all along.

"Come on." Gabriel grabbed Ashliel's elbow and led her to the door. "She's had enough for one day." They left, the door clicking quietly behind them. I heard no key turning in the lock and knew I should flee, but I couldn't make my legs move. I was frozen in shock.

Something wet landed on the back of my hand, and I looked down, frowning when another drop fell on it. Water. Was the ceiling leaking? I glanced up, but there was no leak to be seen. Then I realized it was me. I was crying again; tears were flowing down my cheeks and splashing onto my hands. I couldn't stop them, yet I wasn't sobbing. It was as if my eyes had turned into waterfalls. The tears kept coming and coming, yet I was numb inside. From almost dying at the hands of Michael to Ashliel's betrayal, I wasn't sure I'd survive this day after all—my heart was in pieces. The only thing that kept me going was knowing, somewhere out there, somewhere in the Universe, Levi was alive and waiting for me. I just had to get to him.

EIGHTEEN

The slap on my cheek stung, but I didn't show her that. I'd tried to escape three times now, and Lilith was getting tired of it. This time I'd made it out of the castle and had been halfway down the mountain when one of her dragons had scooped me up and deposited me back to the castle where Lilith had been waiting.

"This is too much, Lucifer," she scolded, fire and ice dripping from her words. "Stop resisting your fate."

"This isn't my fate. I don't believe in fate. I make my own destiny." She hated it when I remained calm, when I showed no emotion. The first time I'd been stopped, I'd been blazing with anger, and it was as if she fed off it. The second time, I'd been desperate, I knew it leaked through despite my best intentions, and she soaked it up like a sponge. I was on to her now, though. This time I kept a tight lid on my emotions, but that didn't mean I'd given in. I'd never stop trying to escape. Never.

"My words will never convince you, but I have something that will."

I studied her face, her skin as smooth as porcelain, poreless and pale, her dark hair and brows in stark contrast. I idly played with the ends of my own hair, knowing I bore a strong resemblance to the woman in front of me.

"And look what you've done to your dress," she admonished, taking in the torn and dirty white dress I'd been wearing for the last three days, my tangled hair still contained twigs and leaves. But I didn't care about the dress, didn't care about anything other than getting out of here. I planned to get as far away from her as possible, so far away that her magic would lose its hold on me—I hoped. For without my magic, I couldn't leave this dimension.

She peered intently at me for another moment before seeming to get tired of the conversation. "Never mind. It's time." With a wave of her hand, my dress changed, my hair fixed, my attitude not.

"Seriously?" For now, I was dressed in purple. Her color. I still wore the white dress, restored to its former glory but over the top a tunic of purple with silver trim. "And time for what?" I asked, watching as the guards at the door pulled it open, and my brothers walked in, followed by Ashliel. The sight of her stung, and my emotions almost fell out. The hurt. The anger.

"Ready, Mother?" Michael asked, approaching her and holding out his arm. Lilith linked hers through it and nodded. They turned and headed to the large double doors on the opposite side of the room, Gabriel linking his arm with Ashliel and falling into step together.

"Bring her," Lilith called, and my arms were seized, and I was propelled forward with a guard on either side.

"What's going on?"

No one answered. We continued in a silent procession, down a hallway, and into a vast, decadent room. The ceilings were at least two stories high, and purple drapes abounded. On a platform at one end sat a throne, gold arms, and back, purple cushions.

"What's this place?" I said more to myself than anyone else.

But Gabriel answered, "The throne room."

Of course, it was. I sighed. All the dramatic flair, the pomp, and ceremony of it all were wearing thin.

Lilith regally made her way up the three steps to the throne, turned, and sat. Michael stood to her left, and Gabriel moved to her right. Ashliel curtsied —*curtsied*—and then settled onto her knees at the foot of the steps. I watched it all with my mouth hanging open. What was going on? Was this some sort of coronation? The doors opened, and people began filing in. I was hustled to the side, my guards keeping a firm grip on my arms, while the room filled, everyone approaching Lilith, bowing or curtsying before moving aside.

Space had been left in the middle of the room, directly opposite Lilith. A second later, I knew why. Guards carried in two clear boxes. In one of them, the Sword of Angels. The other housed the Sword of Souls. I ached to call the Sword of Souls to me, but our connection was blocked, and all I could do was tug against the hands holding me, earning myself an angry reprimand from one of the guards.

Lilith shushed the crowd. "It is time."

"Time for what?" I muttered, flinching when I realized she'd heard me and cast her dark eyes my way.

"It is time to call the witnesses." She smiled triumphantly and nodded at the guards carrying the swords.

"You're down a couple." The words slipped out before I could stop them, but defeating Keres and the Valkyrie had sent them back to their own dimensions, Lilith wouldn't have enough witnesses to do what she planned, and that pleased me.

"Silence!" Evidently tired of my interrupting commentary, a gag appeared over my mouth, pulling tight around my head, and I raised my eyebrows in surprise and challenge. Did she think I'd stay silent forever? True, I was powerless right now, but I was still me. I stood by my beliefs and loyalties, and shutting me up wouldn't change that. I had every intention of escaping this realm as soon as I was able. I had *my* family to get back to.

Using tongs, for only the creators could handle the swords, the Sword of Angels was laid on the floor, then the Sword of Souls laid diagonally over the top. A flash of light shot straight up into the air, dazzling in its intensity, before a display of fireworks that changed into an orb with nine symbols blazing. My eyes widened when I recognized the symbols as the same as the sigils engraved on the Gates of Hell.

One by one, the symbols popped and

disappeared. As they did so, a witness arrived. All-female. All magnificent. Strangers who I'd never seen before, yet on a fundamental level, I knew who they were. Bellona, Goddess of War. Selene, a Moon Goddess. Aphrodite, Goddess of Love. Nut, Goddess of the Sky. Hestia, Goddess of Fire. Gaia, the Earth Goddess. Amphitrite, Queen of the Seas. Freyja, a war Goddess. And Nyx, Goddess of the Night.

"Who has summoned us?" Freyja demanded, "Who dares to call upon us in such a manner?"

"It was I." Lilith stood but didn't descend, standing above the powerful entities in front of her. "Lilith, daughter of the Night."

I blinked. I'd never heard her describe herself that way before.

The witnesses turned in unison and studied the woman who had summoned them. They didn't look happy. Not at all.

"And what makes you think you have the right to call upon us," Bellona, the Goddess of War, drawled, hand curling around the hilt of a sword strapped around her hips. "You are not a goddess."

"I am married to a God," Lilith replied. "I am the wife of Elohim." I couldn't contain my eye roll, to use Dad's name to gather favor was outrageous.

She'd left him and was doing her utmost to destroy him. I tried to speak, but the gag held firm, muffling my words. Still, it drew the attention of the Goddesses gathered, and they all looked at me with great curiosity before turning their attention back to Lilith.

"You bind your own child?" Aphrodite asked, an edge to her voice indicating she was displeased.

"She is yet to learn her place," Lilith replied. "No matter. She is not why I have called you here. I have called the witnesses to rule against Elohim, to take action."

"The accuser is not present?" Hestia looked around. "I have not seen Eli in some time. Why is he not here?"

"I need you to hear my case first." Lilith sounded confident, but I noticed the way she clenched her hands into fists by her side. She didn't like answering to the Goddesses, I realized. But she needed them. Needed them to punish God. I wondered what lies she was about to spin.

"This is a domestic dispute?" Nyx sounded angry, and Selene and Bellona began whispering to each other.

Lilith had the grace to look worried before

smoothing her face back into a neutral expression. "Elohim neglected me. I am his wife, and he neglected me, forcing me out of my home."

"This is not a case for the witnesses. This is gross misconduct of power," Freyja replied, gathering nods from the other Goddesses present.

"I have called you. You must hear me out. It is the law," Lilith said triumphantly.

The Goddesses looked at each other for long silent moments, and I realized they were communicating telepathically with each other. I closed my eyes in relief. They would see through her, see through this pathetic charade, and put an end to it. I would be free. My eyes widened in surprise when Freyja nodded her head,. "Very well. We will hear your case. But Elohim must be present, and he is to be given the same opportunity. His side must be heard. We will then make a ruling."

"But..." Lilith protested.

Freyja cut her off. "That is the law. Do you wish to proceed?"

Lilith nodded, but I could see the tension in her, the way her breaths were coming short and shallow, the bead of perspiration on her upper lip. She had thought to summon all women, to gain favor with them against a man who she believed had wronged her. I had a feeling she was about to be sorely disappointed.

"Very well. We shall summon Eli, and then we will begin."

The women formed a circle and held hands, closed their eyes, and a second later, Father appeared. By his side, Dacian! I choked against the gag, my eyes filling with tears. Dacian was alive. Father had saved him. I stepped forward, but the guards jerked me back into place.

"What is the meaning of this?"

I met Dad's eyes, saw the change in him immediately. He was stronger now; he was back. I closed my eyes briefly, thankful. I wriggled again, wanting to join my father, but the guards held firm, fingers digging painfully into my arms.

Dacian saw and pushed through the circle of Goddesses, sword drawn. "Release her at once!" he demanded.

They didn't. But I felt their hesitation, saw them look to their Queen, and then back at the threat of the angry angel who had a sword resting against one of the guard's throats.

"Do not make me draw blood." Dacian warned,

voice deep and low, the threat genuine. "For this is a fight you cannot win." A second later, the guards released their grip, and Dacian was reaching up to remove my gag gently.

"Okay?" he whispered.

I nodded, my eyes filling with tears again. "You're alive!" I hugged him, my arms wrapping around his neck, tight.

He returned the hug with one arm, the other keeping a firm hold of his sword. "Thanks to your dad. We've been looking for you."

"My magic has been suppressed," I murmured. "I couldn't leave."

"We got the key. Knew you had to be alive," he replied, voice equally low.

But Dad heard us, and he turned to Lilith, his voice shaking with rage. "You took her magic? Her power?"

Lilith swallowed, shifted her weight from one foot to the other. "That's not why we are here!" Her voice went up. "I called the witnesses to hear the case against you. Lucifer has nothing to do with this!"

"Other than you kidnapped me, held me here against my will, and allowed me to be tortured by my own brother!" I shouted, my anger rising.

Startled gasps echoed around the room, and Dad took a step toward her. "You tortured her?" he growled, his voice so menacing even I shivered. I'd never seen him angry. Ever.

"I didn't!" she cried, looking frantically to Michael, who was standing in stoic silence.

"You told him to punish me. He did. You allowed it."

"Punish. Not torture," Lilith corrected.

"So, why have a dungeon? All equipped for inflicting pain?"

"Michael?" Dad cut across us, his eyes drilling into his sons. "Explain."

Michael shrugged. "It's true. Mom said to punish her, so I cut her up. I'd do it again if given a chance." Even though I knew he hated me, the hurt was still fresh, and I winced at his words.

Bellona laid a hand on my father's arm and halted him. "Later," she murmured.

He looked at her for a long moment before inclining his head. "Very well."

"It is time," Freyja decreed, and I swallowed. This was it. Make or break. For Lilith had plotted against my father for millennia, had laid trap after trap for him, I knew she would have prepared for this moment, would present the worst case possible against my father so that he would look guilty, so that the witnesses would side against him. I closed my eyes and prayed.

Lilith's testimony went on and on. My legs ached for standing so long, and I could tell the witnesses were getting restless, too.

Eventually, Nyx stepped forward, hand raised in the universal stop signal. "You are going around in circles and repeating yourself. I say we adjourn for a recess before hearing from Eli."

"But…"

"Silence!" Nyx demanded, voice sharp. "This is a court of the witnesses. Argue with me once more, and you will be in contempt. Not one word from you, we have heard enough."

"We will reconvene in two hours," Gaia decided, and whispers and murmurs spread throughout the room.

Lilith slumped in her throne, her face as dark as thunder about being overridden in her own realm.

Hestia raised her voice to be heard over the noise, "Lilith! We require refreshments. Is there somewhere we can sit and eat?"

Ashliel rose and answered on behalf of my mother. "Yes, of course, anything you desire. Please, come this way to the banquet room. Refreshments are being arranged as we speak."

Leading the way, the witnesses began to follow when Selene stopped and signaled to my father. "Eli? Come. And bring your Angel and daughter. I'm sure their feet hurt as much as ours from standing all this time."

Lilith opened her mouth to protest. When Nyx sent her a look, she quickly snapped it closed again without saying a word. Of course, she didn't want Dad socializing with the witnesses, but not to be outdone, she rose and joined the procession out of the throne room to the banquet room.

Lunch was decadent and plentiful. Platter after platter of roast meats, vegetables, salads, loaves of bread, and fruit filled the massive table we were seated around. Dacian was to my left, Dad to my right, keeping me out of arms reach from Michael, Gabriel, Ashliel, and Lilith. It saddened me that I needed to be protected from family, but it was sinking in that I couldn't consider them my family anymore, for they didn't consider me as such except for Lilith. She still liked to play the mother card, and I heard her drop my name more than once in conversation.

After lunch, we proceeded back into the throne

room, and it was Dad's turn. Thankfully, he kept it brief and surprised us all by agreeing with everything Lilith had said. Yes, he'd ignored her too often—it hadn't been intentional. He hadn't realized it at the time. But rather than talk to him, to explain how she'd felt, she'd left. And he was sorry. He repeated it, his apology was heartfelt, yet Lilith's face remained carved from stone.

And then he told the witnesses all that she had done in retaliation. She hadn't expected it, hadn't expected him to fight, for ever since being released from the tomb, he'd rolled over and let her have her way, feeling bad for hurting her. But not now. Here was the father I remembered. Strong. Fair. Honorable. He accepted his share of the blame for what had happened between them. Now it was Lilith's turn to do the same, but the fury radiating out from her spoke volumes. She did not, nor ever would, take responsibility for her actions against him.

Nut, Goddess of the Sky, delivered the verdict.

"Lilith. Elohim. We have heard your testimony this day, and I'm sure my sister Goddesses agree with me in my assessment." Turning to the Goddesses, in turn, they all inclined their heads toward her, communicating telepathically again. "Elohim," Nut addressed my father.

"Yes, my Goddess." He bowed his head, his respect for her evident.

"We find you not guilty. You have no case to answer this day."

"What!" Lilith screamed, jumping to her feet from where she'd been sitting on her throne, "NO! Not acceptable. He must be punished."

"Silence!" Nut waved her hand, and a gust of wind pushed Lilith down onto her throne. "You imprisoned a God. *A God!* Do you think any of us would allow that to slide? To go unpunished? Do you know what the penalty is, Lilith, Daughter of the Night?"

"W...what do you mean?" She knew then, knew she'd seriously misjudged this particular course of action. She should never have called the witnesses. But it was too late. She had. And she had to obey their decision. Only she'd never thought it would be her receiving the punishment; you could see the panic in her face.

"Death. We could sentence you to death for imprisoning a God," Nut continued, voice grim. I swallowed and looked at Dad, who looked back with a slight shake of his head. What did that mean? That he wouldn't let them kill mom? I wasn't sure how I felt about all of this, but I did know I didn't want her dead.

"However," she continued, "Eli has requested that we spare you, and we will honor his wishes." I closed my eyes and breathed out a sigh of relief.

"Lilith, Daughter of the Night, you are hereby banished to the realm of Toqith. Neither you nor your citizens can leave this place. The door will be sealed forevermore. No one can enter, no one can leave."

"As long as my children, all my children, are here with me, I do not care," Lilith answered. Heads swiveled toward me.

"Oh, I'm not staying. No way. I'm returning to Hell," I said.

"Hell is fallen," Lilith gloated.

"I don't care. I'll rebuild," I argued.

"And I'll help her," Dad chimed in.

"No, that's not acceptable," Lilith argued.

"Silence!" Nut cut her off again. "This is not a negotiation, Lilith. Lucifer is free to leave; she has done nothing wrong in this case. You kidnapped her and forced her to stay against her will. She is free to go if she so chooses."

"I do. Choose to go, that is. And I'd like my powers returned."

"It will be so," Nut assured me with a nod.

"You will regret this," Lilith told me, her eyes shooting daggers. A shiver danced up my spine at her threat.

"Witnesses? We are agreed?" Nut addressed them.

All nine of the Goddesses stepped forward, hands clasped, and said in unison, "By the power of the witnesses, let it be so."

I thought something would happen, something magical, but nothing did. Lilith sat sullenly on her throne. Michael and Gabriel stood on either side of her, Gabriel looked guilty, Michael looked bored, and Ashliel had a new clipboard she was madly typing things into. Out of everything, her betrayal hurt me the most. We'd run Hell together, and aside from Levi, she was one of my closest friends. To learn that it had all been a lie? I lowered my head to hide the tears. I just wanted to go home.

The Witnesses departed, the citizens of Toqith filed out of the throne room, chattering about what had gone down, and Lilith sat on her throne, stunned that none of it had gone her way. That she'd failed.

Catching a glimpse of Ashliel filing out of the room, I hurried to catch up, grabbing hold of her arm to halt her.

"Ash." I didn't know why I'd stopped her. Didn't know what I was going to say. I was still unbelievably hurt by her deception, that our friendship had been a lie.

"You want me to say that I'm sorry, Lucy?" she asked with a familiar arch of her brow. "I'm not. I always thought you were too soft to run Hell. Too fair. Too good. You didn't deserve it."

"I guess we'll have to agree to disagree." I didn't have a witty comeback, barely had words at all for my former friend.

A hand came down on my shoulder, and I looked up to find Dacian by my side.

"Ashliel." He nodded at Ash. "I liked you better as a redhead." Then he steered me away.

"You okay?" he asked.

"I had no idea, none." I sighed, blinking back tears, "I thought she was my friend, I trusted her implicitly, and all along she was spying on me, all along she was..."

"Don't dwell on it. You can't change it, and don't beat yourself up over it. None of us knew. She had us all fooled."

Wiping a tear from my face, I sniffed and then squared my shoulders. It was over. Lilith had lost and was now imprisoned in her own realm, unable to hurt us ever again. It was...surreal. And just when I was settling into my new normal, of being able to breathe and mentally planning the rebuilding of Hell, I felt it. The severing of my connection with Levi.

NINETEEN

I gasped, clutching my chest.

"What is it?" Dacian asked in concern, peering into my face. Panic swept over me, making it hard to breathe, hard to think. I'd lost the connection. He was...gone.

"My bond with Levi," I choked, hysteria building. "It's broken. Gone. I *can't feel him*!" I ended on a cry.

"Okay, okay, calm down."

"Don't tell me to calm down!" I yelled, swinging around in circles, not knowing what I was looking for, not knowing what to do. *What do I do?*

"Lucy!" Dacian grabbed my shoulders and halted me. "Breathe. It might not mean what you think it means."

"What? That he's dead? Why else wouldn't I feel him? Through all of this, despite having my magic locked down, I could feel him. He was alive. And now he's not." I crumpled. We'd been so close, so very close, and now he was gone.

"Remember when he got pulled into another dimension by Zuska, and you thought all was lost?" Dacian reminded me. "We got him back. He survived."

"I wasn't bound to him then. I didn't know. Not for sure."

Dacian pulled me against his chest and dropped a kiss on the top of my head. "Have faith."

"What's happened?" Dad approached, took in my distraught appearance, and addressed Dacian rather than me. Smart man. I was bordering on hysteria. My body was shaking, and I could barely breathe due to the weight on my chest.

"She can't feel Levi," Dacian explained, running a soothing hand up and down my back.

"Come. We shall find him together."

"I can't leave. She suppressed my magic." I sniffed into Dacian's chest, leaning heavily against him. I was tired. Really tired. So tired I could lay down on the floor and die, for, without Levi, I didn't want to continue. I couldn't live my life without him.

"I returned your power, Lucy. You're okay. You're whole," Dad told me.

"Not without Levi, I'm not." And I began sobbing all over again. I thought I heard Dacian sigh, and I tried to pull myself together but failed miserably.

"Don't give up on him, Lucy. Just because you can't feel him doesn't mean he's dead. Something else could be interfering with your connection."

I lifted my head and peered at my father through bloodshot eyes. "You don't think this is one last-ditch attempt from Lilith to hurt us, do you?"

He shrugged. "I wouldn't put it past her. Let's go see, hmm?"

With Dacian holding one hand and Dad the other, we flew out of Toqith and returned to Hell. I felt the tug on my heartstrings that I wouldn't see my brothers or Ashliel again. They'd chosen their paths; this was their destiny, not mine. Then I was distracted by what lay before me as we flew past the Gates of Hell. It was just as I'd left it. Not broken or empty. My two remaining dragons flew above the gate, on guard. And Hell, HQ sat upon the cliff like it always had. It hadn't fallen. And my bond with Levi? It was there, as clear and strong as ever.

"Oh, my Goddess!" I clutched my chest, rubbing at the sweetness of the ache in my heart. It had gone from utter sadness to utter joy so fast it hurt.

"You feel him?" Dacian asked as we materialized in my office.

"I do!" I smiled, my relief bringing tears to my eyes once more. I'd never cried as much as I had on this day. "Let me go find him." I rushed to the elevator since he wasn't in my office. Dacian and Dad were at the monitors, surveying the Earth. From what I glimpsed on the screens, all was well there, too. Amazing. I made a mental note to ask Dad about it once I'd found Levi.

Upstairs I ran through the apartment, calling his name. He didn't reply. He wasn't there, I knew the minute I stepped inside that the apartment was empty, but still, I searched, going from room to room. No Levi. No Mr. Meow. No Nibbler. Where had they all gone?

Anxiety was nipping at my heels when I returned to Dad and Dacian.

"No?" Dacian glanced at my face, then back at the monitors.

"He's not here!"

Dad sighed. "Damn it."

"What?" I seized his arm, forcing him to look at me.

"I think your mother may have boobytrapped Levi."

"Boobytrapped? How?"

"She went to a lot of trouble to make you think Hell had fallen; my best guess is when you returned to this realm, Levi was transported elsewhere."

"To another dimension?" When would this end? The traps and games my mother had planned were mind-boggling.

"I'd say she sent him back to Earth." Dacian was still looking at the monitors. "He's part human. I don't think she wanted him dead, he was no threat to her, plus if she did, she could have killed him and left him here for you to find."

I mulled it over, my eyes flicking over the screens, scanning for signs of Levi.

"I think you're right," I said.

"Dacian, help Lucy search for him. I must return to Heaven, but if you need me, call. I will come."

"Yes, sir."

"Dad?" I hugged him, not sure what to say. He'd answered my prayers, had come to Toqith and rescued me. "Do you know where he is? Can you find him?"

"I wish I could, Lucy, I really do. But since he became part fire demon, I cannot get a firm lock on him, other than he's alive. And I think Dacian is right. Earth is the first place I'd look." He hugged me tightly. "I've repaired what damage I could from Lilith's interference. I've answered prayers, there are many more to go, I've performed the odd miracle or two, and now I need to get back to Heaven and continue my work. You go. Find Levi, I'll send someone to monitor Hell for you, but this is a temporary arrangement—you need to return and take the helm, understood?"

"Yes, Father. I'll return." I knew what he was saying, the hidden words. With or without Levi, my place was here. I could see three of the screens monitoring Hell flashing, indicating trouble was brewing. "I'll sort that out before I go," I told Dad reluctantly.

"I've got it. You go. The quicker you find him, the quicker you will return. I imagine it's only souls kicking up a fuss about their punishment."

"Thank you, Dad," I whispered, fresh tears in my eyes as I hugged him one more time before stepping back and wiping my arm across my eyes.

"Ready?" Dacian asked.

"Ready."

Together we flew to Earth, intent on finding Levi.

WE COULDN'T FIND HIM. I was losing hope when Dacian suggested we check in on the key while we were on Earth. Apparently, they had arrived in Heaven safe and sound, and Dad had returned them to Fury Island.

"They may know something," he suggested.

"Pft, doubtful, but okay. I know I don't have much time, I'm needed in Hell, but I don't think I can face returning without Levi." I admitted my worry for Levi trumped my concern for my own realm.

"We'll find him." He sounded so confident, so sure. I wished I had half of his conviction. My thoughts turned to my mother. She'd done this. She'd taken Levi from me. If I were her, where would I send him? She didn't want to hurt him per se, but she wanted him out of my life, that much was clear. She'd spirited me away to her own dimension and had been intent on keeping me there, away from him. What would I do if I were Lilith?

Flying in low over Fury Island, we came in to land in front of the vet clinic.

"Can you feel them?" Dacian smiled at me, and I beamed in response. Yes! I could feel my bond with the key, and they felt me, for the door flew open, and Del was running toward me, arms outstretched, Duke bounding by her side, barking, and Jase at a more leisurely pace, bringing up the rear.

"You're back!" Del wrapped her arms around me and squeezed, and I laughed, hugging her back.

"I am. Are you okay?"

"We're all good." Releasing me, Del stepped back and eyed me up and down. "And you? What did she do?" Her last words ended on a scowl, and I decided I wouldn't tell them what I'd suffered while imprisoned on Toqith. It would only distress them more.

"I'm good. Everything is sorted. Lilith has been locked in her own dimension; no one can enter or leave."

"I see some amazing things have been happening on planet Earth. All of our people are back," Jase drawled, sliding an arm around Del and tucking her into his side. I remembered then that the entire population of Fury Island had mysteriously disappeared around the same time the Valkyrie had shown up. I made a mental note to thank Dad.

"Yeah, Dad's been busy."

"We met him. Seems a nice bloke."

I barked out a laugh. Typical Jase, laidback as usual.

"I'm looking for Levi. Have you seen him? Heard anything?" I asked. It was a long shot, but I was desperate.

"Oh. You don't know?" Del chewed on her lip.

"Know what? Is he here?" I couldn't begin to hope, but when she nodded, I could have kissed her. Her next words stopped me in my tracks. "There's something you should know, Lucy."

"What?"

"It's Levi."

"What about him?"

"He's…"

"Oh, my god! What? Just spit it out, Del. I can't take any more suspense or drama."

"He's lost his memory. He turned up here, well, not here, not at the clinic. On the dock. We found him on the dock, wandering, dazed, and confused.

He was carrying Nibbler under one arm and another cat under the other, and he was lost."

"What did he say?"

"Nothing. That's just it; he didn't know what he was doing here. He knows his name but nothing else. He doesn't know how he got here. He didn't recognize us."

TWENTY

Flinging open the door to Del's old cottage, I sucked in a breath at the sight of Levi standing at the kitchen sink. He turned and stared at me, then shook his head.

"Look, I know I'm new to Fury Island, but honestly, you people need to learn some manners. Knock first and then wait. Don't just barge in."

Nibbler and Mr. Meow wound around my legs, meowing, and I bent to pat them. I'd missed my furry felines.

"They like you," he noted, standing with his arms folded across his chest.

"You don't know me?" I asked, my eyes drinking in the sight of him, wanting to rush into his arms and hold him close.

"Should I?" There was that brow arch that I loved.

"Yeah, you should. We're mates."

"Mates? As in...friends?" He cocked his head, and I bit back a groan. I'd never expected him not to know me, not to remember. Damn you, Lilith, and your stupid tricks.

"No. Mates as in fated mates. Lovers."

"Oh." His eyes roamed over me, and a bloom of red spread across his cheeks. "Look, I'm really sorry, you're really...pretty...to look at but...I don't know you. You're a stranger to me, and you're telling me we're...what? Married?"

"In a sense."

"Look, lady, we're either married, or we're not." He waved his ring finger at me. "And I'm not wearing a ring, so I'd say not."

"My name is Lucy, and we're bound. There's a tattoo on the back of your shoulder. That's my mark. I bound you to me."

He looked at me with wide eyes, then turned his back, busying himself at the sink. I heard him mutter "psycho" under his breath and sighed. This wasn't going well. I'd barged in and had naively expected that as soon as he laid eyes on me, he'd remember, he'd know who I was. Clearly, that wasn't the case. I needed another approach, fast.

"Levi Forrester. I met you in your tarot reading shop, The Black Hat, in Shadow Falls. You helped me return a soul stealer to his own dimension." I paused, wondering how much I should tell him that he had, in fact, been dragged into the Soul Stealers dimension, and it had taken me more time than I'd have liked to rescue him. I decided to leave that bit out.

"This," I kneeled, and Mr. Meow head-butted my hand, "is your cat, Mr. Meow. Initially, he had no fur because you were allergic. But I healed you and fixed him." I picked up Nibbler and buried my face in her fur, "And this is my kitten, Nibbler. I rescued her here on Fury Island and brought her home with me."

"You healed me? Are you a doctor?"

"Nope." My breath puffed out in frustration. This reminded me of the time in the cemetery in Shadow Falls when Dacian and I had fought. My brothers had wiped his memory; he had no recollection of me at all other than to think I was an evil monster who had to be stopped. I then had a proverbial light bulb moment. I'd kissed Dacian to push my memories into him. I'd do the same with Levi and hope to god it worked.

"You said home…" Levi watched as I rose and slowly walked toward him. "We live together?"

I nodded. "We do." I stopped inches from him and ran my palm across his chest. So hot. My lips curled into a smile when he didn't stop me, didn't move away.

"Do you feel that?" I whispered, unbuttoning the top two buttons of his shirt and sliding my hand in to rest against his flesh. The skin upon skin contact sparked a fire in my veins.

"I feel…" His voice was hoarse. Confused. I saw it in his eyes, the desire burning there, along with the chaos of his current situation.

"It feels good, doesn't it?" I breathed, removing my hand and tugging my shirt over my head, tossing it on the floor behind. My bra followed.

"Er, Lucy, I don't think…"

I cut him off. "Don't think! Just feel. Feel our connection. The chemistry between us. Just feel." I jerked his shirt open the rest of the way, the remaining buttons flinging off and scattering across the floor, fodder for Nibbler and Mr. Meow, who pounced upon them with glee.

Sliding both palms up his chest, over his shoulders, and around his neck, I pressed myself against him, bit back my groan as my blood thundered through my veins, and my skin tingled where we touched. It felt so, so good. His hands moved up of their own volition and wrapped around me, exploring my back as he adjusted to the feel of our bodies pressed together so intimately.

Then I tugged his head down, smiling when he let me, knew he was as helpless as I to resist. My want for him burned. Soon, I knew the fire would be all-consuming, that I'd have no control—I never did it when it came to him—but for now, I had to take it slow. Don't spook him.

His mouth hovered over mine, his eyes blazed with want and need, yet I didn't kiss him. I let our breaths mingle in that space until I couldn't stand it, and I bridged the gap. Standing on tiptoe, I pressed my lips against his, and he groaned, the sound vibrating through me from head to toe. The hairs on the back of my neck stood on end as his tongue swept into my mouth, dueling with mine. I wanted him so badly I could have cried, but my brain was screaming Slowly! Take it slowly! Don't scare him away!

His hands got busy then, cupping my head, tilting me to just the right angle to plunder my mouth, tangling in my hair and tugging before sliding through the strands to wrap around my neck, his thumbs meeting beneath my chin. I was vulnerable but knew this man would not harm me whether he remembered me or not. I had nothing to fear. His fingers lingered on my throat for a second, stroking the skin there before sliding down to cup my shoulders. I couldn't contain the shiver as he explored with exquisite gentleness, familiarizing himself.

"You know me," I groaned, sucking in a breath.

"It seems I do," he ground out, his mouth replacing his hands at my neck, licking, sucking, biting until I was a trembling mess in his arms. It was torturous, going slow, but it was divine torture. Everything around us faded. All that existed was him and me.

As I gazed deep into the dark pits of his eyes, I could see the battle going on, desire, confusion, and something else. I froze in panic. It had worked with Dacian, and he wasn't bound to me. Surely it couldn't fail with this man I loved with all my heart, my soul mate. Lilith couldn't win, not now when I was so close to happiness.

"Levi?" tentatively murmuring his name, the hope in my voice evident.

"Lucy?" He was back. I felt the change in him, knew he'd returned to me, that our connection was too strong to withhold any spell Lilith had placed on him.

"It's okay," I whispered, cupping his face, kissing him. "It's okay. Lilith tried to take you from me, but we're okay."

"We're okay," he repeated, looking a little stunned. "How did I ...? Did you...? What happened?"

"Later," I said. "Right now, I'd like to finish what we started, if that's okay with you?"

He chuckled. "I love you." He wrapped his arms around me, sending a message. We were one.

"I love you, too," I gasped, overcome by emotion. "Always and forever."

And if fireworks lit up the sky over Fury Island to mark our union, good. For everything was as it should be. Levi was back in my arms, the key was safe, and Hell hadn't fallen. All was right with my world. For now, anyway.

Though our journey with Lucy and Levi has reached its finale, the thrill of romance and supernatural suspense continues. Step into the enthralling world of **The Enforcers** where urban fantasy meets passionate encounters and heart-stopping action.

Grab your next romantic adventure here: www.JaneHinchey.com/Enforcers

Thank you for reading! If you enjoyed this book, I'd greatly appreciate your review.

You can find a complete list of my books, including series and reading order on my website at:

www.JaneHinchey.com

Join my newsletter here:

www.JaneHinchey.com/subscribe

And finally, join my readers group on Facebook here:

www.JaneHinchey.com/LittleDevils

Thank you so much for taking a chance and reading my book . It's readers like you who make this journey worthwhile and fuel my passion for storytelling. Your support means the world to me, and I can't wait to share more exciting stories with you in the future.

xoxo
Jane

FREE BOOK OFFER

Want to get an email alert when a new book is released?

Sign up for my newsletter today,

https://janehinchey.com/subscribe

and as a bonus, receive a FREE e-book of

Cupcakes & Curses!

READ MORE BY JANE

Find them all at www.JaneHinchey.com/books

<u>The Ghost Detective Mysteries</u>

#1 Ghost Mortem

#2 Give up the Ghost

#3 The Ghost is Clear

#4 A Ghost of a Chance

#5 Here Ghost Nothing

#6 Who Ghost There?

#7 Wild Ghost Chase

#8 Easy Come, Easy Ghost

#9 Life Ghost On

<u>Witch Way Paranormal Cozy Mystery Series</u>

#1 Witch Way to Magic & Mayhem

#2 Witch Way to Romance & Ruin

#3 Witch Way Down Under

#4 Witch Way to Beauty & the Beach

#5 Witch Way to Death & Destruction

#6 Witch Way to Secrets & Sorcery

The Gravestone Mysteries

#1 Fur the Hex of it

#2 Battle of the Hexes

#3 What the Hex

The Midnight Chronicles

#1 One Minute to Midnight

#2 Two Minutes Past Midnight

#3 Third Strike of Midnight

Clean Scene Inc.

#1 All in Vein

PARANORMAL ROMANCE/URBAN FANTASY

The Awakening Trilogy

Hell's Angel Trilogy

The Enforcer Series (4 books)

Standalones

Returned

Secret Fates

Destiny's Touch

Blood Cursed

Heart of Darkness

ABOUT JANE

Hi there! I'm Jane, crafting tales of paranormal cozy mysteries sprinkled with urban fantasy romance. Between sips of coffee and dodging my mischievous cats, I immerse myself in stories where magic meets everyday life.

Once known as Zahra Stone in the world of steamy urban fantasy, I've now merged those fiery tales under the Jane Hinchey banner. Off the page you'll find me binging on true crime documentaries or sneaking in a power nap. Dive into my stories and join me on an enchanting journey!

Find me here: www.janehinchey.com

facebook.com/janehincheyauthor

instagram.com/janehincheyauthor

amazon.com/Jane-Hinchey/e/B0193449MI

bookbub.com/authors/jane-hinchey

goodreads.com/jane_hinchey